"I love you, Joanna. You. You aggravating, teasing, impossibly lovely witch!"

His kiss was hard, demanding, and Joanna longed to respond. But she was so faint with the shock and wonder of his words that she couldn't. Instead she started to weep from happiness. As the tears ran down her cheeks, he pushed her away.

"My darling, I didn't mean to upset you. I'm sorry!" He looked at her in misery and walked swiftly away.

Joanna stared after him, unable to move, her fingers digging nervously into the pocket of her coat.

And in that pocket was an unexpected piece of paper. She didn't know it was a summons—to disaster!

Also in Pyramid Books

by

Daisy Thomson

MY ONLY LOVE

HELLO, MY LOVE

PRELUDE TO LOVE

BY LOVE BETRAYED

BE MY LOVE

FIVE DAYS TO LOVE

JOURNEY TO LOVE

LOVE FOR A STRANGER

WOMAN IN LOVE

PORTRAIT OF MY LOVE

SUMMONS TO LOVE

Daisy Thomson

PYRAMID BOOKS • NEW YORK

SUMMONS TO LOVE
A Pyramid Book

First published in Great Britain 1971

Pyramid edition published September, 1974

ISBN 0-515-03452-5

Printed in the United States of America

Pyramid Books are published by Pyramid Communications, Inc. Its trademarks, consisting of the word "Pyramid" and the portrayal of a pyramid, are registered in the United States Patent Office.

PYRAMID COMMUNICATIONS, INC.
919 Third Avenue, New York, N.Y. 10022

Chapter One

There was only one letter in the mail that morning, and since I did not recognize the handwriting on the envelope, nor did I know anyone in Inverness where it had been posted, I very nearly left for my holiday in Venice without opening it.

It was possibly some advertiser sending me notice of a bargain sale or a new book offer or some cut-rate motor insurance I decided as I laid it on the table beside my breakfast cup of coffee. Nothing that could not wait until I came home again.

Yet, as I buttered a fresh piece of toast, I found my eyes straying towards it. There was something about the firm, bold handwriting which roused my curiosity. Advertisements are usually typewritten, or penned by an office junior with characterless care.

I hesitated. It might be some outstanding bill I had forgotten about, though why it should be posted in Inverness I could not think. It might even be good news! I smiled at my conjectures. Why not satisfy my innate curiosity by opening the envelope?

I gasped when I read the address of the sender, and was even more taken aback by the message the letter conveyed, and by the clear, bold signature of the writer.

"Dear Miss Frasier," I read. "Your grandfather has been very ill. He has had two severe heart attacks, and a third one could prove fatal. I know he would dearly like to see you and your mother again, but he does not wish to contact you in case he is rebuffed. Why can't you or your mother swallow your damned pride and come to see him?"

The letter was signed "Rory Armstrong."

I expelled a long, slow breath.

The letter brought back many memories, most of them happy, some of them painful.

Sir Hugh Conynghame of Tarris House, Tarrisdale, a small village on the west coast of Scotland is my grandfather.

His only son Ranald had been killed in the last year of the Second World War. My mother, his only daughter, had been widowed a year after her marriage to a test pilot, and had returned to live at Tarris House, where I had been born two months after the death of my father. In fact, I had spent the first seventeen years of my life at Tarris House, and my grandfather had played the role in my life of father-substitute.

We had been very close, my grandfather and I, but he had never spoiled me as grandmother tended to do.

Grandmother was a lovely, serene person, rather quiet and retiring, and the perfect foil for the aggressive, quick-tempered handsome husband she adored.

Her death had been a shock to him, and he had lost much of his fire in the months that followed, so that his decision to remarry, little over a year later, had been a bombshell.

When he had told us that he was planning to marry again, and that his future bride was a widow of forty-seven, sixteen years younger than himself, and the secretary, or some such thing, in a firm in Glasgow with which he did business, my mother was furious.

The fact that the future Lady Conynghame had a son of her own added fuel to her anger.

She told grandfather that he was a silly old man to do what he was doing. No woman of Mrs. Armstrong's age would want to settle down with a man almost old enough to be her father, unless she had an eye to the main chance, and in his case this meant being the titled wife of a county laird of ample means, with an attractive mansion house to call home.

Mother stormed on that she would not live in the same house as a smart adventuress who had so quickly made her father forget her much-loved mother, and grandfather, from whom she had inherited the fiery family temperament, retorted that if she was not willing to accept her new stepmother and give her her rightful place at Tarris House, perhaps it was high time that she cleared out and made a home for herself instead of living off his bounty as she had been doing for the past seventeen years.

One angry recrimination led to another and the upshot was that when grandfather went to Glasgow to marry his widow and take her on a honeymoon trip round the world, mother applied for, and got a job as housekeeper in a large estate on the Borders, with a flat in one of the wings of the house as an added advantage.

She packed all our belongings and without telling anyone of our future destination, she left Tarrisdale "for good" as she snapped to our own housekeeper as we took our leave.

That had been five years ago and not one word had she written to her father since. I too was commanded to keep silent as to our whereabouts, and not to try and get in touch with anyone at home. I found this very difficult, because I had loved Tarris House and the little village of Tarrisdale. I had made many friends in my seventeen years, and I missed them, yet I did what my mother asked me, because I could understand how she felt. Indeed, I was perhaps even angrier with grandfather than she was, because I was a romantic, and could conceive of only one great love in a lifetime, so that I simply could not understand how he could have forgotten grandmother so soon.

I blamed Mrs. Armstrong. Somehow she had twisted an unhappy old man round her finger and made him marry her, but one day he would realize how he had been taken in.

I even envisaged a grand reconciliation when he discovered that mother had been right, and sent the adventuress packing while he sought us out to plead with us to return, but of course this never happened.

Days and weeks and months passed with no news of home and no weakening on my mother's part to get in touch, and when the months grew into years, I decided sadly that there never would be a reconciliation, and that I would never again see Tarrisdale.

Yet sometimes, when the wind blew from the west and brought with it a douce drizzle of rain, a far-away look would come into my mother's eyes and I knew that, like me, she was, in spirit, back at Tarrisdale, and that the drizzle which damped our cheeks was not Border mist, but spindrift from Loch Tarris, and we could almost smell the unforgettable tang of home—the tang of salt water and seaweed and peat reek and the honeyed perfume of the wild broom and heather from the mountain slopes, and like me she must have experienced that almost undeniable urge to return. But she was a Conynghame, and proud as they come. She had made her bed, and she would lie on it, whatever the discomfort.

I graduated from College and started work on a newspaper in Edinburgh, travelling back to our home in the Borders most week-ends.

Then, to my delight, my mother met, and fell in love with the headmaster of a school in the North of England. The announcement of their wedding at the beginning of this week had appeared in *The Times*, and this was the notice which must have put Rory Armstrong on our track.

My reaction to the note he sent me was instinctive. The grandfather I had loved so much, and who had been so good to me was very ill. I had to see him.

I was equally sure that had my mother read

the letter she would have done as I was doing—made arrangements to go at once to Tarrisdale, but she was presently touring the continent on a motoring honeymoon with her new husband, and I had no way of getting in touch with her.

I was sorry about this, both for her sake, and also for my own. The thought of returning to Tarris House by myself was a nerve-racking one, since I had no idea how I should be received either by my grandfather or by the present Lady Conynghame.

I somehow had the feeling that Rory Armstrong, Lady Conynghame's son, had written to me off his own bat, and that it was quite possible that no one else knew about his letter.

I wondered about the letter writer. All I knew about him was that he was a few years older than myself, and that he had been abroad when his mother married my grandfather. From his letter, I also judged that he was a pretty forceful character, who did not mind saying bluntly what he thought.

I was rather shy of telephoning him direct to say that I would come to Tarrisdale this very afternoon, so instead, I sent him a wire. I could imagine how the tongues would wag at the Post Office, and then in the village itself, when they read my message.

"Will arrive home about four o'clock this afternoon. Joanna Fraser."

In Tarrisdale, everyone knew everyone else's business, and I guessed my wire would be the liveliest piece of news they had had for some time!

My bags were already packed for the holiday in Venice which would now have to be postponed, so apart from notifying my friends about my change of destination, all that remained for me to do was to give a glance at the latest road map of Scotland to refresh my memory as to the best way to get to Tarrisdale, before getting into my car and driving north.

Now I was on the last lap of what was to prove the most fateful journey of my life.

I turned off the main trunk road to the north, west to join the minor road, so narrow that passing places had to be signposted, which led to the village where I had been born.

It was the beginning of July, and so warm that I had to wind down the windows of my little Fiat for coolness.

The state of the road, which was badly potholed, as well as a growing reluctance to reach my destination, slowed me from my usual speed, and I was able to appreciate the beauty of the passing landscape.

As I began to recognize familiar landmarks, my pulse beat quickened. Over there was the Cairn of Eagles. To my right was the ruined castle of the Frasers, my namesakes.

The road climbed up from the valley and snaked round the mountainside. On my left a steep slope, still golden with late gorse, dipped down to a fast running stream, which a dozen miles from here would tumble its waters into

Loch Tarris. Beyond the stream, the mountains again rose steeply, gorse and bracken giving way to pine and larch forests, and the forests in turn giving way to scree falls and the damson-purple peaks of the Tarris range.

Towering cliffs on my right rose sheerly from the roadway, which in places had been created by blasting away part of the hillside.

There was a grandeur about the scene which made the rolling hills of the Borders seem douce in comparison, but perhaps it was because this was home that the scenery so appealed to me.

Dark, lowering clouds were beginning to shroud the topmost peaks and at sight of them, I increased my speed. The Black Pass of Tarris is no place to be when a storm brews up, and sudden mists come swirling down the mountainsides, reducing visibility to next to nothing, and I did not wish to join the unfortunate band of motorists who had gone plunging off the narrow road into the rocky gorge far below.

As I urged my little Fiat up the steep climb to the top of the Pass, a cumbersome lorry drew out of one of the passing places ahead of me and lumbered slowly and noisily uphill.

I gave the driver an indignant hoot. With the road behind me empty of traffic for miles, he could have had the courtesy to let me pass before he decided to resume his own journey, since it was obvious that he would hold me back.

To avoid the foul smelling fumes that were being emitted from the lorry's exhaust, I changed down to second gear and slowed down even more, to leave a comfortable distance between my car and it. There was little or no chance of my being able to overtake between now and Tarrisdale, for it was single track all the way, and judging from his action, the driver of the vehicle in front would never dream of pulling off the road into another passing place to give way to me.

It is a long, steep, straight haul up the final hundred yards of road to the top of the Pass, and the mists were growing thicker on the slopes above, and beginning to wisp down to the road itself.

I muttered several unladylike words about the driver ahead, but even these words failed me when, as he was within a foot or two from the top, and driving so slowly that I had had to change down to first gear, the man suddenly jumped from the almost stationary lorry, and ran forward over the crest of the Pass, out of sight, while the heavily laden truck he had leaped from began, at first with a slowness that mesmerized me, and then with a speed which filled me with panic, to come down the long, steep slope towards me!

For a moment my brain went numb. I could not think. Fortunately for me I had not been so close to the lorry's tail as normally I might have been, or it would have been a different story. As it was, the few yards I had fallen behind gave me time to pull myself together, and as the truck came rushing towards me I stopped, and started to reverse downhill as fast as I could. If I could reach the first sharp bend in time, all might yet be well, but luck was against me.

The sheer weight of the lorry added momentum to its downward plunge, and in spite of my best effort, it was now looming almost directly over me.

Somehow I executed one last, desperate manoeuvre. I steered the Fiat as close to the cliff face on my right as possible, so that the side of the car literally scraped the surface of the stone wall. An unexpected outcrop of rock brought the car to a sudden halt. The engine stalled, and as I tried desperately to restart it, the lorry rammed against the near side of the Fiat, and with a vicious, crunching noise, sandwiched it tightly against the mountainside.

The steering wheel was wrenched from my petrified grip. The windscreen shivered into a million splinters of opaque glass, and as I undid the safety belt to slide from behind the wheel as far as possible from the distorting metal, a further jarring movement sent me rocketing sideways. My head hit the pillar of the door with a sickening rap, and then everything went black.

Chapter Two

I thought that I was on a boat, tossing on a choppy sea, and I could not for the moment think how this could be. The right side of my head ached as I opened my eyes and tried to sit up.

"Keep still, lass!" admonished a soft, Highland voice. "We don't want you to move until we get hold of a doctor."

"What happened? Where am I?"

"There was an accident. You are in an ambulance on the way to the Cottage Hospital in Tarrisdale," replied the man, moving into my line of vision.

"You are damned lucky to be alive!" said another voice angrily. "If you had not been on the wrong side of the road, the lorry driver would have seen you, and had a chance to stop in safety, instead of going plunging off the road to avoid a collision. The police are still looking for his body."

"Wheesht, man. Don't upset the lass!" remonstrated the first man, who was small and thin and elderly, and wore the uniform of an ambulance attendant.

I turned my head so that I could see his companion, and found myself looking up into a pair of hazel eyes whose scornful gaze would have shrivelled me if I had earned their contempt.

In spite of the warning, I sat up angrily.

"The police are giving themselves needless work!" I glared back at them. "It was a runaway lorry without a driver!"

The man's thick brows met together in a frown.

"What do you mean?"

"Exactly what I say!" I retorted, pressing a

finger against the spot on my head which was beginning to throb with pain. "There was no one in the lorry. The driver jumped down from his cabin seconds before it reached the top of the Pass!"

"Lassie, lie down!" implored the ambulance attendant, putting a firm hand on my shoulder and trying to make me lie back on the berth.

"Shock!" he added in a knowing tone to his companion.

I shrugged his hand away.

"Shock be damned!" I snapped with exasperation. "I am telling you exactly what happened! I followed that lorry for about a mile after it drove out of one of the passing places ahead of me, until it had almost reached the top of the pass. Then, when it was only a few feet from the crest, it almost came to a full stop. The driver jumped out and ran off out of sight, and while I was still gaping after him, the lorry started to roll back towards me!"

I shivered at the recollection.

"For a second I could not think what to do. Then I put my car into reverse and tried to back down the hill as quickly as possible, hoping to get out of harm's way round a bend before the lorry overtook me, but I didn't quite make it, did I?" I essayed a shaky laugh.

"You did well enough," the man with the hazel eyes was regarding me with interest. "I am afraid your car is a write off, but you seem to have escaped with no broken limbs, as far as we could ascertain, and only a bump on the side of your head to indicate that you were in as nasty an accident as I have seen."

"That lorry driver must have been out of his mind!" said the ambulance man angrily. "Fancy doing a damn fool thing like that, especially when he was bound to know there was a car behind him! Still, we shall have no difficulty in tracing him, and putting him where he belongs. It was one of the County Council Road Department lorries he was driving."

The other man eyed me narrowly.

"Could you describe the man who ran off?"

"Not very well," I shook my head, and gave an involuntary moan as the movement radiated pain from the bump above my right ear right down my neck.

"I think we should let the lass be, and not bother her with questions," said the older man, once more gently urging me to lean back against the pillow. "She will have to tell all she knows to the police later on."

The younger man was still looking at me intently.

"Haven't I seen you somewhere before?" he asked.

I regarded him with renewed interest.

He was broad of shoulder, and I judged him to be a little over medium height. His dark hair was short and wiry, and his skin deeply tanned, indicating that he must have spent a great deal of time out of doors, or abroad. His features were strong and regular, and there was an air of authority about him, as if he was used to command.

He was certainly not the type of man I would have forgotten had I met him, however brief the acquaintance.

I remembered in time not to shake my head for emphasis as I replied.

"I am quite sure that we have never met before. This is my first visit to this part of the world for quite a number of years."

The man frowned and continued to regard me with such intensity that I lowered my eyes and nervously started to play with the dress ring I always wear on the third finger of my right hand. It is a ring which belonged to my grandmother, and which she left me in her will. It is an unusual piece of craftsmanship, a star shaped peridot surrounded by seed pearls in a gold filigree setting.

The fluttering movement of my fingers distracted the stranger's attention from my face to my hands.

He leaned forward and caught hold of my right hand, lifting it up so that he could examine the ring.

"Now I know why your face is so familiar!" he exclaimed triumphantly, and the frown gave way to a smile. "This ring confirms my suspicions. You are like your grandmother, Miss Joanna Fraser. You could well have been the original sitter for that portrait in your grandfather's study!"

Now it was my turn to look puzzled.

"I am Rory Armstrong, Miss Fraser," he introduced himself. "Your grandfather's step-son," he added with an irritating twinkle in his eyes. "I am delighted that you decided to come north so promptly at my request."

I resented his easy air of assurance, and the faintly mocking tone of his voice, and was about to tell him that I wished now that I had never made the journey, but before I could voice my thoughts, he went on.

"All the same, I do wish you had had the sense to give me some warning of your arrival. I had not told anyone at Tarris House that I had been in touch with you, and asked you to come home."

A worried look crossed his face. "If you had arrived without notice, which, thank goodness, I shall now be able to give, it might have been rather awkward."

"But I did let you know that I should be arriving about four o'clock this afternoon!" I protested. "I sent you a telegram this morning, almost immediately after I had received your letter, telling you so."

"Damn!" said Armstrong with vehemence. "It must have arrived after I left for Fort William. I apologize, Miss Fraser," he flashed me a smile which a more susceptible female might have found attractive. "Your wire must be waiting for me at Tarris."

"With most of Tarrisdale knowing its contents before the addressee!" I replied ruefully.

The ambulance attendant interrupted us.

"Of course it's you, Miss Fraser!" he beamed at me. "Fancy me not recognizing you! You came to our house often enough when you and my Elsie were in the Brownies together!

"My!" he went on happily. "It will do Sir Hugh the world of good to see you again. Is your mother coming north as well?"

"She is abroad at the moment, Mr Simpson," I recalled the ambulance man's name. "She will be coming later," I expressed my personal hope.

The ambulance came to a halt outside the little local hospital, and the two men solicitously helped me from it.

Although my head ached and my legs felt like rubber under me, after a thorough examination, Dr Menzies, who had been the Conynghame family doctor for the past twenty-five years, and who had known me since my first breath, and had therefore had no difficulty in recognizing me, informed me that in view of what he had been told of the accident, I was a very lucky young woman to escape with a mere bump on the head and a painful bruise on my ankle where the accelerator pedal had wedged against it.

"You will probably feel slightly shocked for a day or two," he went on, "and I advise you to take things easy for a couple of days. Otherwise, all I can prescribe is an anodyne to lessen the pain in your head if the ache becomes too intolerable."

As he led me from the examination room, Dr Menzies said gravely:

"I am really glad to see you home again, Joanna. Sir Hugh is not at all a well man. This last attack of his was a grave one, and his condition still gives rise for anxiety. He was worried too, about you and your mother, so your coming should set his mind at ease in that respect.

"Thank goodness," he went on, shaking his head, "that this accident of yours was not more serious. Something like that could have a detrimental effect on him, so," he paused, "I do not want you to mention about it to him, and I advise you to warn the rest of the household not to discuss it in front of him."

"I knew grandpa must be far from well when Mr Armstrong took the trouble to write to me," I frowned, "but I did not appreciate just how ill he was. Thank goodness I came home!"

Dr Menzies stopped and turned to me.

"Do you mean to say you did not return off your own bat? That Rory sent for you?"

I nodded.

The doctor pursed his lips.

"That is typical of the man. When he thinks something needs done, he does it, with no beating about the bush."

"Does Armstrong live at Tarris House with his mother?" I asked, wanting to learn something about this new relative of mine.

Dr Menzies shook his head.

"No, no!" he replied. "Rory has a flat in London, but he usually comes north two or three times a year to visit his mother, and he always spends his summer vacations here at Tarrisdale.

That is why he is here now, as a matter of fact. He is fond of sailing and climbing so it suits him perfectly."

Since I made no comment, the doctor went on.

"He gets along very well with your grandfather, too," he eyed me shrewdly. "They seem to have a lot in common. They play chess, and exchange yarns and argue politics, as you used to do with your grandfather, lass. Indeed, I think that young Armstrong has happily filled the blank in the old man's life which your departure from Tarris House created."

"Bully for him!" I sneered. "Like his mother, he obviously knows when he is on to a good thing, and sucks up to grandfather!"

"Rubbish!" said Dr Menzies sharply. "Rory Armstrong is a fine young man, and you have no call to think otherwise."

With an irritated toss of the head, the doctor strode forward down the passage, leaving me to follow.

As we emerged from the corridor which led from the examination room to the main hall, I saw the subject of our discussion lounging against the reception desk, talking to the pretty blonde in charge.

He looked up as we approached.

"Well, Dr Menzies?" he straightened up as we approached. "What is the verdict? Any serious damage?"

Dr Menzies shook his head. "Joanna escaped very lightly, thank goodness, and there is no need to detain her here. Apart from the bump on her head and some superficial bruising there is nothing wrong with her, although I would advise that she take things easy for a day or two."

"Good!" replied Armstrong briskly. "In that case I shall phone my mother and tell her that I am bringing Joanna home with me now, so that she can forewarn Sir Hugh of his grand-daughter's pending arrival."

He turned to the girl at the reception desk.

"Sally, be a dear and put me through to the house, please."

At the mention of the girl's name I turned and smiled at her in dawning recognition, and she smiled back at me as she obeyed Armstrong's injunction.

I had known Sally Henderson vaguely in the past. She was a few years older than me, and in between his more exotic girl friends, my cousin Gavin had always returned to her, in spite of his mother's disapproval, for Mrs Conynghame was a snob, and did not consider the daughter of the local teacher a suitable girl friend for her beloved son.

While Armstrong was breaking the news of my arrival to his mother, the local police Sergeant and a constable, both old acquaintances of mine, arrived at the hospital to take a statement from me about the accident.

Sally suggested that we go into the waiting-room for privacy, and Rory stayed behind to talk to her while I followed the two policemen into the room.

Before we got down to business, the Sergeant told me that all my luggage and personal belongings had been taken from the wrecked Fiat and put into Rory Armstrong's car, to be taken to Tarris House, while the car itself had been towed to the local garage.

He also told me that it was Rory Armstrong who had first come on the scene of the accident.

Apparently Rory had been on his way back to Tarrisdale from Fort William when he had seen the lorry go plunging over the side of the roadway into the gorge. He had stopped his car and climbed down the steep cliffs to go to the aid of the driver, but when he had failed to find the man in the cabin of the truck, he had hurried back to his car to notify the police in Tarrisdale of what had happened.

It was not until he had rounded the bend over which the lorry had toppled that he had come on my wrecked car.

Because of the way the Fiat was squashed up against the cliff face, with its near-side badly damaged, he had been unable to pull me out, and rather than move me forcibly in case I might be seriously injured, he had resumed his race to the village to urge the police and the ambulance to come to the rescue.

Then the Sergeant asked me to tell him exactly how the accident had happened.

When I finished my account of the affair, both men looked thoroughly puzzled.

"The driver must have thought he was not going to make it over the top, and panicked!"

The Sergeant shook his head. "There is no other explanation!"

My head was beginning to ache again, in spite of the pills Dr Menzies had given me, and I must have looked as weary as I felt, because the Sergeant stood up and said:

"We shall not keep you any longer, Miss Fraser. From your description of the man, and also being able to check who was driving that particular lorry today, we should have no difficulty in getting hold of him, but if we need to get in touch with you again, we know where to find you."

He ushered me from the waiting-room into the hall and added:

"Please give my regards to Sir Hugh, Miss Fraser. Tell him we all hope that he will be well enough to open the library extension next month."

With a smiling farewell to Sally, Rory came forward to lead me out to the yellow Lotus Elan which was drawn up in the hospital forecourt beside the white police car, and as the officers gave us a farewell salute, he opened the passenger door of his car and helped me inside.

Chapter Three

"You will be glad that that interview is over," said Armstrong as he slipped into the driving seat beside me. "Have they managed to get hold of the driver of the lorry yet?"

"No, but they don't expect to have any difficulty in picking him up."

Rory switched on the engine. "I still cannot think why he did such a damn fool thing. He must have had a brain storm."

"The police think he panicked because he thought the lorry was not going to make it over the top."

"Could be," shrugged Rory as we left the car park and drove down the High Street, past the harbour, to turn left at the church for the long, winding climb to Tarris House, which stands high up on the side of Mount Tarris, on a promontory having a commanding view of the Loch.

The dull aching pain at the side of my head became more pronounced, and as we negotiated the first of the hairpin bends, my hands involuntarily clutched at the base of the seat for support, in case I gave it a further bump as we swerved round.

To take my mind off the twisting roadway, I glanced sideways at the man beside me.

A lot of women might find him attractive, I conceded. His craggy features, his magnificent suntan, the charm of his smile and even the subtle aura of being a man used to command were all factors which made up this attraction.

He certainly did not look the type of man who would trade on an old man's affections, but at college and in my present job I had come in contact with many men, and learned that you cannot always judge a person by his face value.

Dr Menzies had not mentioned whether

Armstrong was married or not, but I deduced from the fact that since he seemed free to travel north from London whenever he felt like it; since he owned a car which could by no stretch of the imagination be termed a family runabout, and since he did not seem to be averse to Sally Henderson's charms, judging by the way he had been chaffing her, he must be a bachelor.

Indeed, it might be his friendship for Sally, rather than his duty as a son, which brought him north so regularly.

Armstrong looked into his driving mirror and caught my eye.

"You are very quiet, Miss Fraser, or perhaps I should get used to calling you Joanna?" He gave me a quick smile. "Are you feeling all right, or is your head still very sore?"

Swiftly I averted my curious gaze from his face and fixed my stare on the road ahead.

"I am afraid my head is beginning to ache again." I closed my eyes against a particularly acute spasm.

"Did Dr Menzies give you anything to take for the pain?"

"Some pills. But it is too soon for the next dose."

"Poor girl!" he said sympathetically.

"It could have been worse," I tried to sound bright. "I really was lucky to escape from an accident like that so lightly, wasn't I?"

"We make our own luck," said Armstrong firmly. "You used your wits to try to get out of a tight corner, so you earned your luck."

I felt ridiculously pleased at the implied praise and was immediately annoyed with myself for feeling the pleasure.

Rory Armstrong was a practised charmer, I told myself, but I was not going to be taken in by his flattery as my grandfather had been, both by him and his mother.

I pursed my lips primly together and Armstrong, who had been watching me in the mirror, frowned and said:

"Joanna, are you sure you can't take anything else for your head? You don't want to arrive at your grandfather's looking like a woebegone orphan of the storm! He will start to worry about you, and that won't do him any good."

"You do think he will be pleased to see me?" I blurted out the other worry which had also been giving me a headache.

"So that is what it is!" Rory heaved a sigh. "You are wondering what sort of reception you are going to have at Tarris, is that it?"

"Well—" I hesitated.

The man's brows met in a frown.

"I can assure you that your grandfather will be delighted to see you," he said slowly. "As for my mother, in spite of the way you and your mother snubbed her, you need have no worry about the way she will receive you. She has always had your grandfather's best interests at heart, and knowing how he has pined for a sight of you, she will welcome you to her home," he stressed the last two words.

I was about to snap back that Tarris House

had been my home for seventeen years, and that it was his mother who was the intruder, but with an effort I managed to bite back the angry words. Such an outburst would have spoilt any hope of a reconciliation, and in any event, Armstrong's words had at last brought home to me the truth. The second Lady Conynghame was as much the chatelaine of Tarris House as my grandfather's first wife had been.

I stared silently ahead of me, and Rory made no further attempt at conversation.

Thunder which had been muttering in the distance ever since we had left the hospital, grew louder. Great black storm clouds which had been looming over the horizon were now closing in on us, creeping down the mountain-sides and blotting out the sun.

A sudden squall of hail swept across the roadway, peppering the windscreen of the car with such force that the wipers could scarcely cope with them.

The road had levelled off slightly, and Armstrong accelerated. As the extra power surged through the car, my head ached with even greater intensity, and I was relieved when I caught sight of the long, high wall which surrounds Tarris House.

We were almost at journey's end.

A couple of hundred yards further on I could now see the break in the wall where it curved into the driveway. My heart began to beat faster with anticipation. Minutes now, and I should see my old home and my beloved grandfather once again.

We were only yards from the entrance gateway when a jagged flash of lightning seared across the faces of the stone gryphons which topped the gate columns, giving them such an evil, menacing look, that I shuddered.

"Scared?" asked Armstrong in surprise.

"No!" I shivered again. "A goose over my grave."

"That usually presupposes disaster, doesn't it?" he said. "In this case, I think the goose has come too late. You have had your accident!"

I essayed a shaky laugh, but the chill feeling of premonition I had had lingered in my bones.

As Rory slowed the car and changed down to take the sharp turn into the driveway, above the growling thunder we could hear a fierce klaxoning. Next moment a grey Jaguar came speeding out of the driveway, its tyres screaming in protest as the driver made a sharp, skidding turn into the roadway.

Armstrong veered swiftly to the left as the Jaguar went racing past us, and I had to snatch at the grab handle to prevent being flung against him by the sudden manoeuvre.

"Exit Lois!" Rory grinned. "How that young woman has not had an accident I shall never know! Gavin should have more sense than to lend her his car."

"Don't tell me Gavin is here too!" I exclaimed in delight. "That is a nice surprise!"

Armstrong shot me a swift, curious look.

"He lives in Tarrisdale permanently now, didn't you know?"

"Why, no! Has Gavin's father retired then?"

"You are out of touch!" Rory was genuinely surprised. "Your grand-uncle died last year, in the 'flu epidemic, and when the old manse near Tarrisdale harbour came up for sale, his widow bought it and brought Gavin back here with her."

I looked at him in bewilderment.

"But what on earth is there for Gavin to do in Tarrisdale? When I was here last, he was talking of emigrating to Australia after he took his degree in agriculture. That is why I was so surprised when you said he was here."

"His mother soon quashed that idea!" said Rory.

Knowing what a domineering and possessive person my great aunt was, I could understand how the easy-going Gavin had fallen in with her plans.

"Moreover," went on Rory with the trace of a sneer in his voice, as we reached the point in the driveway where the lines of tall cedars which flank it gave way to a thick hedge of rhododendrons which stretch the final few hundred yards to the flagged courtyard of Tarris House, "she has ambitions for her son. As you must know, Gavin Conynghame is your grandfather's titular heir, being the only other male member of the family. She believes that with you and your mother in Sir Hugh's black books, her dear son stands a very good chance of inheriting the estate, together with a handsome legacy to keep it going. Believe it or not, she has even talked your grandfather into giving Gavin the job as factor, now old Mackenzie has retired!"

He grinned suddenly.

"You know, Joanna, somehow I do not think that she will be at all pleased to see you back here again! You might spoil her plans!"

I did not pay much attention to what Rory was saying.

All I could actually think of was that Gavin was here, in Tarrisdale; Gavin, who was the only son of my grandfather's younger brother, and who was a mere four or five years my senior; tall, good-looking Gavin, whom I had idolized as a teenager, but who never noticed me, any more than he noticed the familiar furniture about the place, because there were older, prettier girls in the district practically queuing up for the honour of being dated by him; Gavin, who spent his money like water on fast cars and expensive clothes, and who could afford both because he could always wheedle extra cash from his over-loving, over-possessive mother.

I took a swift glance at myself in the driving mirror.

In spite of my recent frightening experience, I did not look too bad. My brandy brown hair had a silken sheen, and now there was a sparkle in my cat-green eyes.

I was a little pale, perhaps, but my skin was clear and smooth, and although my dark brown silk blouse and brown trousers were still slightly dusty as a result of the smash, their tailored neatness flattered my slim figure.

I had come a long way in the right direction since I had last been overlooked by Gavin. Surely this time he would take notice of me, I thought hopefully.

Chapter Four

I sat in the car for a moment or two, gazing up at Tarris House.

The storm had passed, and the late afternoon sun was reflected back with dazzling brilliance from its tall, narrow windows. Round the massive porch, with its Doric columns and thick oak door with its cast iron hinges, two climbing roses were in full bloom, and their branches, heavy with blossoms, met in a solid mass of scarlet under the carved stone shield on which the Conynghame coat of arms and motto were depicted.

These roses had not been planted in my time, and I had to admit that their rioting colour softened the harshness of the dark grey sandstone from which the house had been built, and gave a feeling of warm welcome.

A bed of roses had also been planted round the house, under the windows, and as I stepped out of the car, I could smell their fragrance.

I wondered what other changes had taken place here since Rory's mother had become mistress of the house, and I clenched my hands so tightly in dread of these changes which might spoil my memory of my old home, that my fingernails dug painfully into my palms.

While I stood looking about me, Rory lifted my cases from his car, and strode off towards the house. I followed him, still nervously clenching and unclenching my fists.

Had I been right to come back? Did my grandfather really miss me as much as Rory had made out?

Sudden shyness made me want to turn tail and run, and if I had had my own car, I think I would have gone racing back down the driveway, away from Tarris House and the strangers to whom it was now home, but as it was, there was no going back for me now, so I squared my shoulders, and held my head proudly high as Rory pulled the great chain which would set a bell resounding throughout the hall and servants' quarters, and waited for his imperious summons to be answered.

It was Mrs Oliver, the housekeeper who had served at Tarris for as long as I could remember, who opened the door.

Her beaming smile of welcome reassured me that here at least was one person who was glad to see me again.

"It's yourself, Miss Joanna!" she held out her hand to shake mine warmly. "We are all so happy that you have come home again!"

She blinked away the emotional tears which had gathered in her eyes.

"You have no idea how delighted your grandfather is at your home-coming. I haven't seen him look so like his old self for months!"

She ushered me into the vestibule, with its sturdy stands for sticks and fishing rods, and its walls adorned with antlers and stagheads and the old, damp-spotted prints depicting the original House of Tarris, as it had been in the early nineteenth century, before successive owners had added a wing here and a turret there, making it into the long, rambling pile it was today.

The west-wing, which had been allocated to my mother when she had returned home as a young widow, had been added at the end of the nineteenth century and was a complete house in itself, although it was connected by an upper passageway, which could be locked off, to the main building. This wing jutted right to the edge of the promontory, and had a wonderful view over Loch Tarris.

I was glad to see that nothing at all had been changed in this outer hall. The stuffed golden eagle still stood poised for flight in the niche above the entrance to the main hall, and on the weathered oak table to the left of the door, the two small alligators which my grandfather had brought home after a visit to Australia still bared their teeth with the vicious look which had terrified me as a child.

It would seem that although the new Lady Conynghame had altered the plan of the garden, she had left the interior of the house unchanged.

But I was as wrong about this as I was to be about a great many other things in Tarrisdale.

Mrs Oliver opened the door into the main hall and stood aside to let me enter.

I stepped forward a few paces and then stopped, taken aback by the transformation.

The main hall of Tarris is octagonal, and completely panelled in pine wood. Opposite the entrance door, a great, wide staircase leads up to the half landing, which is lit by a ceiling high stained glass window, with gorgeous blue and golden and crimson clad figures carrying sheafs of lilies, which are the family emblem.

At the half landing, the stairway divides, with one stair leading left and the other right, to the upper storey, where a balcony encircles the well of the hall, and off this balcony are the main bedrooms and the corridors which lead to the rest of the house.

In my day, the glass dome which forms the ceiling of the hall had been painted over, a relic of the war-time blackout, and the pinewood of the walls and staircase had been covered over with a dark brown varnish, giving the place a dark and gloomy air.

Here and there along the panelled walls, portraits of vapid-looking Conynghames of the past, painted by inferior artists, had been hung, and the entire floor area of the hall had been covered by a carpet so elderly that the pattern had been worn away except in a few odd corners.

Now the paint had been removed from the glass dome, so that you could see the sky above, and the varnish had been stripped from walls and staircase, exposing to view the true beauty of the light pinewood.

The insipid portraits had been removed, to be replaced by two magnificent seascapes which I had never seen before, but which I recognized immediately as views of Loch Tarris. The worn carpet too had vanished, the parquet floor it concealed had been sanded and polished, and in the centre of the hall, directly under the dome, a circular glass table, on which was set a crystal vase of the red roses from the porch, stood on a circular Chinese carpet of a rich, deep, delphinium blue.

The old Japanese screens behind which I had played as a child, the lumpy Chesterfield suites which had been set around the enormous fireplace in the left wall, and the many occasional tables had all disappeared, and now there was only one comfortable-looking suite, upholstered in velvet of the same shade as the carpet.

Even the fireplace was different. The antiquated gas fire had been taken out, and a pile of logs, ready to be set alight, rested in the fire basket.

"There have been a few changes since you left, Miss Joanna," Mrs Oliver smiled at the look on my face. "All for the better, too, as you will agree. It is ever so much easier to keep the place clean when it isn't all cluttered up."

My emotions were confused. I had loved the hall as it had been—dark and sombre and mysterious, with a wealth of hidey holes for a child to play in, and yet, if I would let myself, I could be delighted with its new look, if I did not identify this new look with the woman responsible.

"It's a big improvement from when I saw it first," said Rory bluntly, when I made no comment. "I think that mother and Lois have made a wonderful job of the place."

Lois. I frowned as I heard this name for the second time since my arrival at Tarrisdale.

Who was this Lois? What was her connection with Tarris House?

I was still frowning when I heard the soft click as the living-room door was opened.

I turned round, and came face to face with the second Lady Conynghame for the first time.

Chapter Five

I had been seventeen when my grandfather remarried, and a romantically inclined, impressionable young girl.

Mother had spoken of Mrs Armstrong as an adventuress and a schemer; a gold-digger who had taken advantage of an old man's loneliness to obtain a pleasant home and a very pleasant social position for herself.

The only facts I had known about her were that she was a widow, only a few years older than my own mother, that she had a son in his twenties, and that she worked with a firm in which my grandfather had a business interest.

I had combined fact and opinion in my head to conceive of her as a hard-headed, determined ambitious woman. The woman who was now advancing towards me may have had some of the qualities I had attributed to her, but in appearance she was pleasant to look at.

She wore a lambswool jumper and skirt of deep, cornflower blue, which exactly matched her amazing eyes, and her shortish grey hair was brushed back from her forehead in soft waves.

There were tiny wrinkles at the corners of her eyes and mouth, but otherwise her smooth skin was unlined. There was a youthful air of vitality about her, an easy grace in the way she moved, which reminded me of her son.

Lady Conynghame took my outstretched hand and held it for a moment in a cool, firm grip.

"So you are Joanna!" her mouth smiled, but there was a wary look in her eyes, as if she was assessing what my reaction to her was going to be. "I expect you are tired of being told how like your grandmother you are?" Her eyes lingered speculatively on my face.

"It's just the colouring." I gave a nervous laugh.

There was a moment of silence. Lady Conynghame seemed as much at a loss for further words as I was.

To break the moment of awkwardness I said hurriedly:

"How is grandfather? Does he know I have arrived?"

Before replying she turned to the housekeeper.

"Mrs Oliver, I know you have made some of your special tea cakes for Joanna, and I am sure that she will be ready for a cup of tea to revive her after what she has been through."

She dismissed the housekeeper with a smile, and when the older woman had disappeared into the corridor which led to the staff quarters and kitchen, she turned to her son.

"Hugh is sleeping at present, and I don't want to waken him until I know more about this accident you referred to on the telephone, and also the reason for Joanna's unexpected return."

She crossed to the log fire in the hall, and motioned me to sit down on one of the chairs drawn up beside it, while she bent down and put a match to the pile.

Rory set my cases down at the foot of the staircase and came over to join us.

"I sent for Joanna," he answered his mother's second question. "I thought it was high time the stupid family feud was over and done with. Life is far too short for such childishness, and I knew, from what he told me, that Hugh was anxious to see his daughter and grand-daughter again, but was frightened to get in touch with them himself, in case he was rebuffed. I also knew that it was out of the question for you to get in touch with them, so I did the obvious thing."

He looked at me, a smile in his hazel eyes. "I must say I admire the way you replied so promptly."

"So am I!" said his mother softly. "Joanna,

the telegram you sent to my son was telephoned direct to the house from the local Post Office, and I took the call. When I told your grandfather at lunchtime that you were on your way, it was wonderful to see the way his face lit up."

"Oh!" I beamed with pleasure. "I was afraid he might still be annoyed with us. In fact," I confessed, "several times en route I nearly lost my nerve and turned back."

Lady Conynghame bent down to fan the fire, which was beginning to smoulder into life, and I noticed that her hands were shaking slightly as she asked her next question.

"And what about the accident, Rory? You were telephoning from the hospital. I recognized Sally's voice when she put me through. Who was hurt, and how was Joanna involved?"

Briefly Rory told her what had happened.

His mother frowned.

"I wouldn't be surprised if it was Harry Brook who was in the lorry. He has been acting queerly of late, and drinking far too much. There was talk of dismissing him at the last Council meeting, but he has been a driver with the Road Department for so long, no one seems to want to take the final decision."

She gave me a worried look. "I am glad you escaped as lightly as you did, Joanna. If anything had happened to you, especially when you were on your way to see your grandfather, the shock could have had serious consequences for him."

"I don't think he should be told about it,"

said Rory. "No. On second thoughts, perhaps it would be wiser to mention that Joanna was involved in a minor mishap. In that way, should anyone talk of an accident to him, he will already have accepted our version and not ask further questions."

I looked at Armstrong with respect for his sensible assessment of the situation, and found myself wondering what sort of job he did, and if it was one in which his swift judgements would be appreciated.

"How is the head now?" he asked me. "Do you think you should take another of these pills the doctor gave you, before you go to see your grandfather?"

"I shall take one with my tea," I said, as we heard the squeaking wheels of the tea trolley which Mrs Oliver was pushing into the hall.

"Mrs Oliver has prepared your old bedroom in the west wing for you," said Lady Conynghame, "so I hope you don't mind the smell of turpentine, Joanna."

I looked puzzled, and Rory explained.

"My mother is an artist. Didn't you know?"

I shook my head, and my eyes strayed to the two magnificent seascapes which hung in the hall.

Rory nodded. "Yes, these are two of her paintings. Loch Tarris fascinates her, and she has painted it in most of its moods. She has converted what was the nursery in the west wing into a studio, hence the smell of turpentine."

"I thought you worked in an office before you married grandfather!" I blurted out.

Lady Conynghame smiled. "I worked in the design department of Springfields. Commercial art offered a more stable income for a widow with a child to bring up than the occasional sale of a painting. Now," she sighed happily, "I can paint what I like, and I don't have to worry whether it will sell or not!"

The doorbell rang.

Rory rose to his feet and went to answer it, and left alone with his mother, I was at loss to know what to say.

"I shall pour you a fresh cup, Joanna, if you want to take the pills Rory was talking about," she suggested. "Your grandfather will wake up any time at all now, and be eager to see you, so you want to be feeling your best, don't you?"

She handed me the cup, and I was swallowing the pills when Rory returned, followed by three visitors.

The first of the new arrivals was my aunt, or more correctly, my great-aunt, Morag Conynghame.

Morag is overpowering both in build and in manner. She used to pride herself on doing physical exercises to keep herself in trim, and now she moved towards me with the same old vigorous swing. I had always been a little in awe of her, although she tried to hide her militant personality with a gushing, girlish manner, for I had learned in the past that underneath the effusive façade lay a domineering and determined character.

From the way he had talked to me about her, I knew that Rory Armstrong had formed the same opinion of Morag, and I wondered if this opinion was based on his own or his mother's experience of her. I also wondered how the two women got on together. In spite of their very different exteriors, were they two of an ambitious kind?

As my aunt came hurrying towards me she held her arms outstretched in a melodramatic gesture of welcome, but her eyes did not quite meet mine as she clasped me in a light, perfumed embrace to which I meekly submitted.

"My dear Joanna!" she exclaimed. "What a wonderful occasion this is!"

She released me, and as she stepped back, her keen eyes took in every detail of my appearance.

"You get more and more like your dear grandmother," she darted a sideways glance at Lady Conynghame to see how she reacted to this remark, but grandfather's wife was looking at her son and appeared not to have heard.

Morag now addressed her directly.

"Well, Phyllis, what has Hugh to say about the return of one of his prodigals?"

"Hugh is naturally delighted," said Lady Conynghame smoothly, and turned to smile at the woman who had followed Aunt Morag into the hall.

I had never met this stranger before, but I knew, without being told, that this must be the

Lois that Rory had spoken of earlier that afternoon.

She was tall and slim, with deep brown eyes and a smooth, white skin which emphasized the lustre of her eyes and the jet blackness of her silky hair, which was coiled in a plaited bun at the nape of her neck.

Her tailored costume was of very fine, clerical grey worsted, and must have cost more than my month's salary, and the same could be said of the black leather handbag she carried. A triple rope of pearls adorned her neck, filling the bare V of the suit, and my first thought was that a man would need a fortune to keep Lois in the luxury to which she was accustomed.

Lady Conynghame introduced us.

"This is Lois Burgess, Joanna," she said, "and Lois, this is Sir Hugh's grand-daughter, Joanna Fraser, or do you two already know each other?"

Lois held out a languid hand.

"No, we have never met," she said as her hand touched mine in the briefest of contacts. "Although father has his law practice here, after he and mother were divorced, I lived with mother in England for most of the time. It is only since her remarriage I have come to spend my holidays here," she drawled, as she appraised me from head to foot.

"However, I am spending all of my time here now," she glanced meaningfully at the third of the new arrivals, who was coming forward, smiling broadly, to meet me.

I held my breath with sudden shyness as Gavin stood in front of me, looking at me with blatant approval, a twinkle in his flirtative eyes.

"Welcome home! Joanna Fraser!" He salaamed deeply. "A hundred thousand welcomes!"

His clowning relieved the rather strained atmosphere which had been building up, and what did it matter if Lois Burgess did not look too pleased at the way Gavin was regarding me?

"Gavin!" I returned the affectionate kiss of greeting he gave me with warmth. "It is good to see you. And you haven't changed at all!" I added with a mischievous smile.

"If by that you mean that I could never resist an excuse to kiss a pretty girl, you are quite right," he smiled gaily, while his eyes lingered admiringly on me. "How come I never noticed how pretty you were before?"

I laughed. "You were too busy noticing my friends!"

"I shall have to make up for that, won't I? How long are you home for?"

"I am not very sure," I hesitated, and looked towards Lady Conynghame, but she did not notice, and appeared to be listening to a bell which was tinkling from a nearby room.

"Hugh must be awake," she turned to me.

"I converted the old living-room downstairs into a bedroom for your grandfather, Joanna. It makes it so much more convenient for everyone. So, my dear, run along and see him now. I shall join you in a few minutes."

I excused myself to the others, and rather

shyly walked towards the room from which the impatient ringing of the handbell could still be heard. I entered, and closed the door quietly behind me.

Grandpa was sitting propped up by a number of pillows in a high bed which faced the window.

He was very much thinner than when I had last seen him, and his thinness made his sharp features look even more hawklike. His still thick hair was snow white, and his hand on the little handbell was gnarled, and blue-veined and bony looking.

He had not heard me come in, and as I self-consciously approached the bed, I said hesitantly:

"Hello, grandpa!"

He looked round quickly. His keen gaze rested for a long moment on my face, and then he said, his lips widening in a smile of welcome:

"Joanna! My dear, dear child!"

I crossed the remaining yard which separated us with a joyful stride and gripped the hand outstretched towards me in both of mine.

"Grandpa!"

I bent over and kissed his cheeks.

I was half laughing, half crying as I hugged him, and he stroked my hair and murmured once more, "My dear, dear child!"

After a time, he pushed me gently away.

"Now, stand back and let me see you, girl," he said, with some of his old, authoritarian manner.

I stood up and took a pace back.

"Ah! That's better!" he smiled, and his eyes once more studied me.

"You haven't changed much, Joanna, have you? You have lost your freckles, and you seem taller, but that's all."

He raised himself a little higher on the pillows.

"Now tell me. How is your mother, Joanna? I have been so weary for news of you both!" he sighed.

"Did you know mother had married again?"

He nodded. "I saw the announcement in the paper."

"You will like Angus, her new husband," I said, sitting down on the edge of the bed, and still holding his hand affectionately. "He and mother are ideally suited, I should say. Angus is a schoolmaster, used to handling obstreperous youngsters, and mother," I smiled. "Well, she hasn't changed a bit! She still flies off the handle easily—you know whom she inherits her temper from—and my step-father can soothe her ruffled feathers in an instant! Yes," I mused, "I am sure they are going to be very happy, but you will see that for yourself," I went on confidently. "Now that I have broken the ice by coming home again, I am sure it won't be long before she follows my good example!"

He squeezed my fingers.

"Dear Joanna, you cannot know how happy you have made me today. Five years is a long, long time."

He closed his eyes and leaned contentedly back against the pillows.

I watched him tenderly, and when his head drooped, and his grip on my hand relaxed, I gently eased my fingers free, and crept from the room.

Chapter Six

When I emerged into the hall, Mrs Oliver was wheeling away the tea trolley. I looked around to see where the others were, and intercepting my glance, the housekeeper said:

"Lady Conynghame and her guests have gone upstairs to the studio. Miss Burgess was eager to see her latest painting. It is one she wishes to give to her father for his birthday."

"Does Lady Conynghame sell her paintings?" I asked in surprise.

Mrs Oliver nodded.

"She held an exhibition in Inverness last summer, and sold a number of them to American buyers. Mind you," she shook her head. "Don't get any wrong ideas about this. Lady Conynghame paints for pleasure, but at the same time, she would be daft to pile her canvases out of sight if there are people to whom they would give pleasure and who are willing to pay good money for them, wouldn't she, now?"

"I suppose so," I frowned. "But what has grandfather to say about it?"

"Sir Hugh is very proud of her success. It was

his idea in the first place to hold the exhibition. But you will have to excuse me, Miss Joanna. Lady Conynghame thought it would be nice to give a little dinner party to celebrate your home-coming, and she has invited your Aunt Morag, Gavin, Sally Henderson and Miss Burgess and her father to come for a meal at eight o'clock, so I shall have to go and tell cook."

She bustled off, and I went hurrying up the stairs and along the windowless corridor which had been made from a series of roomy cupboards, to lead to the west wing.

The heavy door which divided the main house from this adjoining wing was closed, and I had to give it quite a vigorous pull to open it.

I smiled to myself. This at least had not changed from the old days. The door had been continually sticking, but the local joiner had said that it was a combination of the thick carpet, and damp occasionally swelling the jamb, which caused this, and if we wanted the corridor draught free, there was not much he could do about it.

As I approached our old suite of rooms, I could hear the sound of voices in what had formerly been my nursery-playroom.

The west wing has four bedrooms and a bathroom upstairs and two public rooms, a large kitchen and a laundry downstairs, and is in fact a very compact house in its own right, with a spacious hallway and cloakroom and a front door leading into the grounds.

Mother had converted the largest bedroom

into a playroom for me when I had been a child, because its windows faced north and west and it was light and bright and airy.

I was not surprised that Lady Conynghame in turn had wished to convert it into her studio, because apart from the question of light, the room, being on the gable end of the house, which is built right out on to the promontory, commands superb views from both its windows of Loch Tarris and the mountains beyond.

I joined the others in the studio, and in reply to Lady Conynghame's questioning look, I told her that grandfather had fallen asleep again, and so I had left him to enjoy his rest.

"Hugh still tires very easily," she nodded. "But he is growing stronger each day. By the time your holiday here is over, I am sure we shall see a big difference in him."

I was curious to see more of Lady Conynghame's works, and crossed to admire the one which was standing on the easel when Lois Burgess decided it was time she went home.

"If I have to persuade my father out of his chair in front of the fire and the television, and get him to change to come here for dinner at eight, I had better get a move on!" she averred.

She turned to Gavin and said imperiously.

"You will call for us about quarter to, won't you, darling? I hate the way daddy drives, and he won't let me touch his funny old buggy."

Gaven looked uncomfortable.

"Sally hasn't got a car, Lois, and since she lives next door to us, it would look churlish if I left her to walk up here," his voice tailed off. "I mean," he hesitated. "Well, your father is not exactly small, and it would be a bit of a squeeze for three in the back of my car."

Lois looked momentarily disconcerted. Then she spoke in one of those over-sweet voices which convey the feeling that the speaker is anything but sweet in mood.

"Of course you could not possibly let poor little Sally walk. I shall suffer the eccentricities of my father's driving in a good cause."

"It is all right, Gavin," put in Rory. "There is no need for you to worry about transport for Sally. When mother telephoned to invite her to dinner, she told her that I would call for her."

Lois smiled with sly triumph.

"Good. Now that that is settled, I shall be on my way. I'll see you tonight at eight o'clock, Lady Conynghame," she addressed her hostess.

"If you can wait a second, Lois, I shall give you a run home," said Gavin.

"No need to put yourself out on my account, darling," Lois smiled at him. "As it is, I feel like some exercise after being cooped up in that dusty old office of father's most of the day. I shall take the short cut through the wood."

She turned back to Lady Conynghame. "By the way, I hope those papers I brought you a little while ago are in order. Typing is not exactly my strong point."

"At least you can spell, Lois," laughed my grandfather's wife, "and that is more than could be said for your predecessor."

Lois took her leave and Gavin and his mother followed shortly afterwards.

Rory lingered on to help his mother stack away the canvases she had been showing to Lois, and I was about to excuse myself, when Lady Conynghame, after directing Rory where to place the paintings said to me:

"Joanna, I am so glad you have come home. Wasn't it worth the effort to see your grandfather's delight?"

She sounded sincere, and I felt myself warming to her.

"Yes. He was so pleased to see me! The look in his eyes told me more than words could say, that I had been right to come back."

I looked at Rory.

"Thanks for sending for me," I said simply.

He smiled, and again I realized how charming this young man could be. "Thanks for coming."

"The doctor is still worried about Hugh," frowned Lady Conynghame. "To begin with, I was not at all pleased when I heard you were on your way. You see, I have been told to keep him from being over excited, and I thought your unexpected arrival might upset him, but now I know that Rory was right, when he says that good news harms no one."

"Doesn't grandfather ever get restless, having to lie still for so long? He was always such an active person."

"I try to sit with him as much as possible," said his wife, "but in a house of this size, there is always something to do, and of course, I have very little time to paint at the moment." She sighed. "Lois does not understand why I have not been able to finish her picture for her, but this studio is so remote from the rest of the house, I don't like to be here, in case Hugh should want me in a hurry."

"Now that Joanna is home, she will be able to keep grandfather company and let you have an occasional break," said Rory firmly. "I have to confess that that is another of the reasons I sent for her. The way you are going on, with so little sleep, I realized I had to do something drastic if I did not want to have two invalids on my hands!"

"I'll do anything to help you, Lady Conynghame," I said eagerly. "Please tell me what I can do. I want grandfather to get well again as soon as possible."

She smiled. "I am sure you do, Joanna. And now, I shall tell you the first thing you can do!"

"Yes?"

"You can stop calling me Lady Conynghame!" she said firmly. "It makes me feel as if we are mere acquaintances and not members of the same family."

I looked at her.

"I can hardly call you grandma!" I expostulated, and Rory let out a whoop of laughter.

"You asked for that one, Phyllis!" he grinned at his mother. "Grandma Conynghame! I never expected to hear you called that!"

"You ought to!" she riposted. "At your age, it is high time you were married and settled down, and presented me with a grandchild to keep me youthful."

"You know me," he said lightly. "I am not the marrying kind. Unless, of course, I could persuade Lois to look my way!"

"You know perfectly well Lois has eyes for no one but Gavin," said his mother sharply. "I want no more family upsets."

"Nonsense! There is nothing like a spot of competition," teased Rory. "In any case, don't you think this 'understanding' is wishful thinking on Aunt Morag's part? Lois is the only girl Gavin has gone with to date, of whom she has approved."

He turned to me and proffered me a cigarette, which I refused.

"Beware of matchmaking mothers, Joanna!" he warned me. "Or perhaps yours is of the same ilk?"

"I am only twenty-two!" I protested. "I have no intention of marrying and settling down for years! I want to make a name for myself as a journalist first!"

"Don't tell me you are not even engaged!" he teased me. "A lot of girls I know would think they had been left on the shelf if they did not at least have an understanding with some man."

"No engagement, no understanding, only ambition!" I said lightly. "I am sorry to disappoint you."

"You don't disappoint me!" Rory looked at me in such a way that I felt my cheeks begin to crimson, and I hastily turned away and spoke to his mother.

"Ollie said that dinner would be at eight o'clock, and I should like to unpack my things and put them away before then. Do you mind if I do that now, Lady Conynghame?"

"Not Lady Conynghame, please!" she reminded me. "And certainly not Grannie either!" she added with amusement. "Rory calls me Phyllis, so I don't see why you shouldn't do the same."

I went to my room and started to unpack slowly.

From the studio next door I could hear the murmur of voices, and a few minutes later the muffled sound of steps as Rory and his mother walked along the corridor past my bedroom door, on their way to the main building.

They were rather pleasant people I thought to myself. When Rory was not being authoritarian as he had been earlier in the afternoon, he could be very charming.

Charm. That was a quality which both mother and son possessed. Now I could understand why my grandfather had remarried, and I could well believe that Rory must have broken a few hearts in his time. What was more, they both appeared to be genuinely fond of my grandfather, and if they had had faults, for this reason I would have overlooked them.

I sighed happily to myself as I opened my cases. It was good to be back at Tarris House, and the return had not been anything like the ordeal I had expected it to be.

It took me longer to decide what to wear that evening than to hang away my clothes. Most of the garments I had with me had been packed with a view to spending a holiday under a hot Italian sun, and were not quite the thing for a cool, Scottish summer.

With evening there had been a change in the weather. The blustery wind of the afternoon had dropped. A mist had crept down the mountainsides and across the loch, right to the promontory on which Tarris House stands.

As I looked out of the window I could see it swirling in odd, wraithlike shapes, like malevolent witches waiting to enshroud some miserable mortal, over the narrow pathway beneath me. In seconds, even the frail rail which guarded the side of the path from the sheer drop of the precipice, which plunged right down to the rocky shore, was hidden from my view.

There was an uncanny quiet, as if the mists had absorbed all sound, and with a shudder I stepped back from the window and hurriedly pulled the curtains across it, to hide the grey world outside.

In my bedroom, I felt as isolated as a prisoner in solitary confinement. The west wing is so remote from the rest of the house, that not even the cheerful clattering noises from a busy kitchen, nor the movements of other members of the household disturbed the silence.

It had no doubt been thoughtful of Phyllis to let me have my own bedroom again, but at the moment I would much rather have been in the main house, within shouting distance of a fellow human being!

I sat on the edge of the bed and began to roll a gossamer thin pair of pantihose up my legs.

An unexpected, loud, creaking sound from the passageway outside made me start, and poke a nervous finger through the nylon.

I stood up, holding my breath, listening for a repetition of the noise, but all was quiet once again.

I gave a shaky laugh. What had I been expecting? The furniture and fabric of any house creaks from time to time. My nerves must be in a bad way to let my imagination play havoc with them, making me fancy that someone, or something, was creeping stealthily along the carpeted corridor, on malice bent.

In spite of this appeal to my logic, I still could not dismiss my unease. It would seem that I had not come out of the afternoon's accident as lightly as I had thought. I must now be suffering from delayed shock.

I took a deep breath and tried to pull myself together. I simply must try to conquer these odd, nervous sensations I had been having. It would never do to let grandfather suspect all was not well with me.

I discarded the torn nylons. I had only packed two pairs, for there would have been little need of them in Italy, so I put on the second pair with especial care.

The dress I had decided to wear was of fine angora wool in a subtle shade of greyish pink, like the feathers in a pigeon's breast. It had a gold chain belt, and I put on a pair of high-heeled sandals of gold leather.

Because Gavin would be at the dinner party I took especial pains with my make-up. In fact, I took such a long time over this part of the proceedings, it was almost eight o'clock before I was ready to go down to join the rest of the party.

I hurried along the corridor, and tried to push open the door to the main wing, but I could not get it to move.

I tried several times to push it open, but in vain. I knocked loudly on the wood, and shouted, but no one heard me. Not that this surprised me, because by this time everyone would be downstairs, ready to enter the dining-room.

I bit my lip.

Would someone come to fetch me, or would Phyllis think I had decided to be awkward by not turning up at the party she had arranged for my benefit?

Angrily I gave the door another violent shove, but still it failed to budge a single millimetre.

I wasn't completely stuck, because there was nothing to prevent me going down the stairs of the west wing, out of its front door, and along the narrow path which skirted the house, and led along the promontory to the main entrance. Only the thought of the swirling mists outside made me hesitate.

I knocked and shouted once again, but the only answer was a mocking echo of my own voice from the corridor behind me.

So that was that. However misty and miserable it was outside, I should just have to go that way. With growing irritation I hurried to the stairway and down to the front door.

To my surprise, the door was unlocked, but then, even in my day, when this wing had been in constant use, we had rarely locked this door at night. Tarris House is at least two miles from the village, and its high walls and long driveway don't make it an attractive proposition for casual thieves.

My high heeled sandals made haste difficult, and I was picking my way with care down the steep flight of steps, already made slippery by the damp mists, which led from the porch to the pathway, when disaster overtook me.

On the second step I tripped over what must have been a trailer from the creeper on the wall. With a frightened scream I went stumbling forward, off balance, down those steep steps, to the narrow path below, knowing that all that could stop me from a fatal dive over the precipice on to the rocks far below, was a thin, single, rusting rail.

I screamed once more as I hit this rail with a force which dislodged one of the stanchions, and sent its cemented base crashing downwards, and then I fainted.

Chapter Seven

Someone was calling me. The anxious voice seemed to be coming from a great distance, down the corridors of a dream.

I stirred and opened my eyes.

"Joanna!"

I looked up and there was a man with dark, angry eyes and an unsmiling face bending over me. A dark lock of hair tumbled over his forehead. I was still half dazed, not sure if I was asleep or awake, and the worried look on the man's face puzzled me.

"What on earth are you doing here?" I murmured, and put up my hand to brush back the recalcitrant tress of his hair.

"Joanna!" The voice was harsher now, the arms in which I felt myself lifted strong, and the buttons of the jacket against which I was held so sharp that they dug through the fine wool of my dress into my flesh, rousing me to complete consciousness.

Memory of what had happened returned.

"Oh, Rory!" I whimpered, and clung for comfort to the stalwart figure. "I thought—oh God! I thought I was going to go right over the edge!"

"You are all right now, Joanna," he spoke firmly. "You are quite safe."

"Rory, it was awful!" I still clung to him as if he was a lifebelt in a stormy sea. "There was something across the top of the steps, and I tripped over it, and came headlong down—"

"It is all right, Joanna," he repeated, as he carried me back up the flight of steps, into the house, and up to my bedroom, where he set me gently down on the bed.

I shuddered once more and he looked down at me and took my hands in his, and gently rubbed the warmth back into them.

"I am not surprised you tripped," he shook his head. "These shoes you are wearing are damned stupid ones to go walking in. Haven't you any sense?" he chided me.

Two great tears welled into my eyes.

He pursed his lips and said fiercely. "You little idiot. You could have killed yourself—and not only yourself." He glared at me. "What do you think the shock of anything disastrous happening to you would do to your grandfather?"

Anger can be contagious.

"If someone had done something to keep the door in the corridor from sticking, I would never have had to use the front way out!" I snapped. "And if I hadn't been afraid I might upset your mother by not turning up for her dinner party, when I found I could not get the corridor door to open, I might have stayed on in my room and gone to bed. I am more in the mood for a quiet evening after the accident this afternoon, than for making bright conversation!"

As he automatically continued to chafe my hands with his warm, strong fingers, Rory frowned and said:

"I have told my mother several times that something should be done about that door. The carpet keeps riding up and sticking it. At least that is what happened tonight, as I discovered when I came to see if you were all right when you had failed to put in an appearance downstairs."

He caught his lower lip in a puzzled grimace.

"As a matter of fact, a large bead had got wedged under the carpet, so all your pushing would never have opened the door from your side. I wonder how it got there?"

"And I wonder why no one sees to it that the creepers round the front door are properly trimmed and not allowed to trail dangerously across the steps!" I retorted, still feeling indignant. "Does no one use the main west wing entrance nowadays?"

"Very rarely," replied Rory, "so it was just as well I decided to come and fetch you tonight. When I couldn't find you in your room, I realized you must have decided to leave by the front door, and I came down to see if I could make up on you."

"I am glad you did!" I exclaimed. "I might have lain on the path unconscious for ages, getting chilled to death!"

"You might," he agreed sombrely. "Yes, it was just as well I decided to come and find out what was keeping you. I was pretty sure that you would not want to miss the party," he stopped rubbing my hands, although he still held them, and there was a mocking glint in his eyes as he went on:

"After seeing the way you greeted him this afternoon, I did not think that you would want to miss the opportunity of having a further chance to flirt with your dear Gavin!"

I tried to pull my hands from his, but he held them too firmly.

"But it is no good, Joanna, let me tell you. Lois has her eye on him. That girl has more enchantress's wiles than any other woman I know, and she is determined to keep Gavin at her beck and call."

"Are you another of her willing slaves?" I asked with a sneer.

He grinned teasingly.

"I am a gentleman, Joanna. I prefer blondes!"

He let go of my hands so suddenly that I almost fell backwards.

"Now you had better hurry, my dear," he said lightly, "or there will be a search party out to look for us. It is quarter of an hour since I told mother to serve another round of drinks while I came to fetch you."

I stood up, and noticed for the first time a great, brown, rusty stripe above the waist of my dress, made by the impact of my crash against the guard rail.

"I can't go down like this!" I said.

"No," his eyes narrowed. "That would never do. I don't want anyone to know what happened to you tonight, do you understand? Phyllis has had enough upsets for one day."

"And so have I!" I exclaimed. "I want to put these accidents out of my mind and not talk of them again."

I crossed to the wardrobe and pulled out a sleeveless sheath of a dress of brilliant, psychedelic colours, a whirling mixture of purples and blues and pinks and oranges, which would have looked all right under a Mediterranean sun, but seemed rather garish for Tarrisdale.

"Do you think this will brighten up the party?" I asked, beginning to feel more myself again.

Rory's eyes gleamed.

"You certainly won't pass unnoticed," he grinned. "Shall I go out while you change?" he added impishly.

I flung the hanger at him, and he laughingly retreated.

"I shall wait for you outside the door," he said. "To make sure you arrive safely this time."

It did not take me many moments to whip off one dress, put on the other after quickly washing the moss stains from my hands and the knees of my nylons. I ran a comb through my hair, dabbed on a little fresh powder and lipstick, and although I did not feel quite as elegant as I had hoped, I was decidedly lighter of heart as I went to join Rory and go with him to meet the dinner guests.

"I am sorry I kept you all waiting," I smiled apologetically as I crossed the hall to where they were sipping pre-dinner drinks in front of the blazing pine wood fire. "It has been one of those evenings!" I went on to explain. "I laddered one pair of nylons and had to unpack to find a fresh pair—" I shrugged.

It was the truth, but not the whole truth, and if Phyllis Conynghame's quick glance towards Rory showed that she suspected this, his bland reply that I had also had some difficulty in doing up the zip of my dress and he had arrived at a timely moment to help me, seemed to settle her doubts.

Rory strolled across to the glass-topped table to pour me out a glass of Tio Pepé, while his mother introduced me to Lois Burgess's father, an elderly man with a receding hairline, an increasing waistline, and one of those sorrowful looking faces with flabby dewlaps and baggy eyes, who greeted me jovially and said:

"It is good to see you back in Tarrisdale, Miss Fraser. I am sure Lois will be glad of your company while you are here. She finds it very quiet after her exciting life in London, don't you, my dear?" He turned to his daughter.

Lois smiled smugly.

"Tarrisdale has its compensations." Her eyes flickered momentarily in Gavin's direction, but Gavin was looking at me and not Lois.

"You are looking very bright and gay tonight, Joanna!" His eyes approved of my choice of dress. "No one would think you had been involved in this spectacular crash everyone is talking about."

"I heard about your accident," Lois surveyed me with her cool, clear eyes. "What exactly happened? I know that a lorry went off the road, but someone said you went into the cliff on the wrong side. Did you panic or something?"

"I certainly did not!" I retorted with heat. "It was the Road Department lorry driver who did that."

"Oh no it wasn't!" interjected Mr Burgess. "I meant to tell you, Lois, but you were too busy beautifying yourself to listen. I dropped into the local on my way home tonight, and there I heard that the police have already got in touch with the man who usually drives that lorry. He swears he had nothing to do with the crash. He said someone pinched his lorry when he left it unattended for a few minutes, but he hadn't reported the matter to the police, because he thought it was one of his pals playing a trick on him, and he didn't want to get him into trouble."

Phyllis Conynghame looked doubtful.

"That doesn't sound a very likely story, does it? Wouldn't you say he had made it up to talk his way out of trouble?"

Burgess shook his head.

"I am inclined to believe him. Half the village knows where Harry Brook parks his lorry in the afternoon when he is supposed to be up at the quarry. In fact, it is a wonder that Ken Mackay hasn't found out before now about his wife's affair with Brook."

Gavin added water to his whisky.

"I don't know about that. Mackay is away from home most of the time, and when he is here, who would talk to him about it? He isn't particularly friendly with anyone in Tarrisdale."

"And small wonder!" said Sally. "The man is a brute. The way he beats Molly up when he is in a rage is quite dreadful. Why he is only fined, and not sent to prison for these assaults I cannot understand." She shuddered. "I hate to think what he will do to her when he finds out about Harry's visits."

"I wonder if Brook will drag her in to alibi for him?" I asked. "He doesn't really need to, does he? He could make up several reasonable excuses for leaving the lorry unattended without mentioning her name."

"But would the police accept an excuse, without a witness to prove that what he said was true?" asked Rory.

"There's always Holy Willie," I suggested. "If Brook left the lorry anywhere near the Mackay house, he would be sure to have noticed it. That is, if he is still alive, and still living in that old shack of his in the woods?"

I put down my sherry glass, and refused Rory's offer of another drink.

"That's an idea, Miss Fraser," nodded Burgess. "I wonder if the police have thought about Holy Willie? It is amazing what that old rascal sees!"

"Who on earth is Holy Willie?" asked Phyllis.

"Don't tell me you have lived in Tarrisdale for five years and never come across him!" I said with surprise.

"He is one of the local characters," explained

Burgess. "He is a religious fanatic who preaches hell and damnation to whoever will listen to him. He lives in an old forestry hut near the Mackay's house. It is almost falling to pieces, but is held together by the texts he nails round the walls!" he joked grimly.

"I can't say I have ever come across him," said Rory.

"He hasn't been so active of recent years," said Sally. "Almost the only times I see him in the village nowadays is on a Tuesday when he goes to the Post Office to collect his pension and to do his week's shopping." She shook her head. "He is a poor old soul, and I feel very sorry for him, although as a child, he used to frighten the life out of me!"

"I am surprised he has not denounced Molly to her husband as a Scarlet Woman before now!" said Gavin. "I thought such an accusation would have been right up his street, and he is bound to know what is going on."

"I shouldn't be at all surprised if he takes a perverse delight in the situation," suggested Sally. "I know for a fact that Mackay tried to get the Council to put him out of his shack and have him committed to an Institution. When one of the doctors from the hospital went to see him about it, old Willie invoked every curse he knew on Mackay's head, and he probably thinks that what is happening now is an answer to one of these invocations!"

Mrs Oliver came to tell us that dinner was ready to be served, and to my relief we stopped talking about the afternoon's incident, and its possible repercussions, and went into the dining-room.

Chapter Eight

The dining table at Tarris House is round, which makes conversation among those seated at it much easier to listen to.

I was placed between Gavin and Rory, with Sally on Gavin's left, next to Phyllis. Lois was on Rory's right, with Mrs Conynghame between her and her father.

Lois was looking extremely lovely and sophisticated in a black velvet dress with a wide boat neckline. She wore no jewellery save for a magnificent Spanish comb with a glittering crescent of diamonds, which held her sleek black hair in a coiled bun on top of her head. It was small wonder that Sally kept darting envious glances at her.

Phyllis looked tired and spoke very little during the meal, but Gavin's mother made up for this.

She kept plying Mr Burgess with questions about some tricky legal point or other which she could not understand, but her conversation had no interest for me, and I paid little attention to what they were saying.

I was delighted that I had been placed next to Gavin, and in no time he and I were happily chattering away, recalling old times and places and people. Sally joined happily in our small talk.

It was fun remembering incidents from the past; old romances and old jealousies; old friendships and old enmities, and in time I was brought up to date with what had happened to former friends and acquaintances.

The meal passed quickly, and after coffee had been served, at Phyllis's suggestion, I went to grandfather's room to say goodnight to him, leaving Gavin and Sally still talking animatedly about the good old days, and Rory flirting gaily with Lois, who seemed to prefer his company this evening to that of Gavin.

Grandfather was looking quite bright when I went into his room. He asked me to sit with him for a few minutes, so that I could tell him more about what mother and I had been doing since we had left Tarrisdale, and from the way he spoke, I sensed how eager he was to see his daughter again.

He was extremely interested to hear about the profession I had chosen to enter, and asked some very pertinent questions about it.

After half an hour, Phyllis came in and tactfully suggested that I should rejoin the others, while she gave her husband his medicine and settled him down for the night.

I was feeling rather tired myself by this time, and hoped the party would not go on for much longer. My head was beginning to ache, and I found it rather difficult to concentrate on the conversation.

Lois had pointedly annexed Gavin once again, and Sally was trying to persuade Rory to give her a helping hand with the shooting gallery she was hoping to have for the local Garden Fête the following week.

Aunt Morag was chattering to Lois's father about some connection she had read about between the Conynghame family and a ducal house in Spain, which had inferred that the Conynghames were entitled to use a grandee title, and she was wondering to whom she could apply to find out more about the matter.

Mr Burgess, slightly glassy eyed after the excellent meal and rather too many glasses of Talisker, the potent and uniquely flavoured malt whisky of Skye, to which he had surreptitiously been helping himself from time to time, went into a long rigmarole about heraldry and the Lyon King of Arms, and as his voice droned on monotonously, I settled back wearily in the comfortable chair near the fire, and concentrated on the difficult business of politely remaining awake.

I was doing my best to stifle a yawn when Sally happened to glance in my direction. She gave me a quick, sympathetic smile, and to my thankfulness turned to Phyllis and said:

"It has been a very pleasant evening, Lady Conynghame, and I should love to stay longer, but I am on early duty tomorrow morning. Will you excuse me?"

"Of course, my dear!" Phyllis glanced at her watch. "Heavens!" she exclaimed. "I had not realized how late it is! I am sure you must all be ready for the road!" she tactfully indicated to her other guests that it was time to go.

"No point in you having to drive down to the village again, Rory," said Gavin, when the women had gone to get their wraps. "Sally can easily squeeze in between mother and me in the front seat."

Then he turned to me. "By the way, Joanna, how about coming round the estate with me tomorrow? There is a lot I want to show you."

Lois, who was hovering in the doorway as Gavin was speaking to me, did not look at all pleased at this suggestion, and I wondered if she would try to talk him out of it on the homeward journey.

When all the guests had departed I offered to help Phyllis with the tidying up, but she looked at my tired face and chased me off to bed.

As is usually the way when one is overtired, I could not fall asleep. Disconnected thoughts kept crowding my brain. I began to worry about a number of things. What should I do about my car. Was it a complete write off, or could it be mended locally? And what did I do about the insurance? Would I need to get a police report about the accident before I could claim?

And my mother. What would she have to say about the accident to the car, towards whose payment she had contributed? And what would she say about my coming back to Tarrisdale? Would she be annoyed or pleased? Would she think that I had taken advantage of her absence to go sneaking back home behind her back?

In the small hours of the morning small worries take on major proportions. One thought led to another. I had had two near fatal accidents within twenty-four hours. Twice I had nearly gone to my death over one of the steep precipices of the Tarris mountains.

A cold sweat broke out over my whole body. Things usually go in threes. What had fate in store for me next?

I tossed and turned, but each time I was on the point of falling asleep an odd groan from the furniture, a stealthy scraping behind the wainscot, the eerie hoot of an owl from one of the outbuildings, or the weird moaning in the chimney of the gusting wind would rouse me to full consciousness once more.

I tried to think of pleasant things. My grandfather's delight in seeing me again; the kindness his second wife had shown me when she could so easily have been indifferent; the fact that Gavin Conynghame, my adolescent idol, was actually here, in Tarrisdale, and that the passing years had not made him any less attractive to me, although, from the occasional looks he had sent me during the evening, the years seemed to have made me more attractive to him.

I smiled a smug little smile. Gavin had certainly not been as attentive to Lois Burgess this evening as from her possessive attitude and Phyllis's earlier remarks, I had expected him to be, and, my smile grew even smugger, he had asked me to go out with him the following afternoon.

Even if our date was only to let me see the things he had been doing to the estate, it was always a beginning, I decided, and there was so much of Tarris to see, I should be able to make the afternoon spin out for a good few hours!

Gavin had always enjoyed rambling round the extensive estate, and although it had never been his home, he knew a great deal about it.

Grandfather, especially now that he was ill and could not attend to the place himself, must be pleased and relieved to think that his nephew was giving Tarris his personal attention.

Rory, in his cynical way, might think that Gavin had an ulterior motive in concerning himself so much with the management of the estate, but why shouldn't he? Gavin was a Conynghame, after all, and Conynghames had concerned themselves with the running of Tarris for centuries.

It was Rory Armstrong who was the outsider at Tarris.

Rory. I frowned. How far had this man, with the mocking smile and the bland charm which he could turn on at will, insinuated his way into grandfather's affections? Sufficiently to ensure that he and not Gavin would inherit the estate?

At one time, my mother and I would have been the natural heirs, but with his remarriage, and considering the way we had walked out on him, it was more than likely that he had altered his original will and named new heritors. Naturally his new wife would be one. Was Rory with his expensive taste in cars, and his freedom to come north to stay at Tarris whenever it pleased him, another?

What did Rory work at? I still had not found out. It was of the man who had arrogantly summoned me to return to Tarris House, and not of Gavin Conynghame, that I dreamed about when I eventually fell asleep.

Chapter Nine

Someone was nudging my shoulder. Impatiently I shrugged off the pressing fingers as I stirred from sleep, and rolled over into a more comfortable position on the bed.

Once again a hand grasped my bare shoulder and I was shaken gently.

I sighed sleepily and reluctantly opened my eyes, and there was Phyllis Conynghame standing at my bedside, smiling down at me.

"You looked so peaceful that it seemed a shame to waken you, Joanna," she said.

I stifled a yawn and wriggled up from the sheets to a sitting position.

"Morning!" I mumbled sleepily. "I am sorry if I have slept in."

"You haven't really slept in," she said pleasantly. "It is only nine o'clock, but Hugh, who has been awake for hours, keeps asking to see you. You don't mind getting up now, do you?" she pleaded.

"Of course not!" I assured her, stretching my

limbs to waken me. "I don't really like a long lie."

Phyllis went over to the side table.

"I hope you prefer coffee to tea," she went on, lifting a tray from the table and carrying it across to me. "I have a percolator in the studio, and a toaster grill, for handiness when I am working there, so I prepared your breakfast there to save time."

As I took the tray from her, she looked at me.

"By the way, Joanna, I should like to ask a favour of you."

"Yes?" I wondered what was coming.

Phyllis hesitated. "My dear, I know that you consider this to be your very own bedroom, and that you must still think of the west wing of Tarris as home, but, well," again she hesitated, "you are rather a long way from the rest of the household here, as Rory pointed out to me this morning, and it would really make it much easier for Cherry, our daily, and old Mrs Oliver, if you would stay in one of the guest rooms in the main building.

"You do understand, don't you? There would be so much less fetching and carrying for them to do, and"—her voice trailed off as if she was seeking other adequate reasons, before she added, "I would much prefer if Cherry did not have to come through to this wing. Although she is a good worker, she is inclined to be nosy, and I don't want her to poke round in the studio."

After last night's incident, and the restless sleep I had had, I was only too pleased to have the opportunity to move from the lonely wing to the main house, and I replied with alacrity.

"I don't want to put anyone to extra trouble on my behalf, Phyllis. I shall be only too pleased to occupy whichever room suits you best for the rest of my stay here."

She looked relieved.

"In that case," she said, "once you have had your breakfast and gone to see your grandfather, I shall arrange to have your belongings packed and taken to the turquoise room. You know the one I mean?"

"The room on the left at the top of the main stair," I nodded. "But I shall take my things along there myself. There is no need to give anyone else the extra task."

I poured myself a cup of coffee, and Phyllis sat on the end of the bed and continued to chat.

"Do you know, the turquoise room is one of the few rooms of which Lois approved when I showed her round the house. How she itched to get her fingers on to altering things!" She shook her head. "Lois is very talented in her line," she idly traced the pattern on the bedcover with her forefinger, "but some of her ideas are more suitable for very modern homes than for a place like this."

"I gather that Lois is an interior decorator, or something of the sort?" I said as I buttered a piece of toast. "What made her come back up here?"

"Lois was doing very well with a firm in London," I was told, "but then, something went wrong. I believe the company went bankrupt, something like that, although she never told me the full details. She tried several other firms, but in a specialized profession like that, there are always too many people chasing too few jobs, and she could not find one which suited her. London is an expensive place to live in if you don't have a job, and her father suggested that she come home and work with him until something else turned up."

Phyllis stood up and crossed to the window. "What turned up was Gavin. They were mutually attracted to one another, and I think she has now given up all thought of going South again. After all, if they are going to get married, it is hardly worth while to start on a new venture in London, for she will have enough to do here, finding a suitable home and doing it up as she wants it done."

"Gavin is always being attracted by pretty girls," I said quickly, "but nothing ever comes of it. Are you sure he is serious about Lois?"

"Gavin is five years older than when you knew him before, Joanna," Phyllis reminded me. "Now that he has settled permanently in Tarrisdale, it is only natural that he should think in terms of marriage. He is twenty-eight, you know, and Lois would make him a very suitable wife. She is clever and attractive and would fit well into local society. Moreover," she turned and smiled at me. "Morag approves of Lois as a potential daughter-in-law, which is quite something, and I think that Mr Burgess would be very happy to have his daughter staying near him. Because of the divorce, he has seen very little of her until now."

"You speak as if everything was cut and dried!" I protested. "Yet they are not even engaged!"

"According to Morag, they have an understanding and are merely waiting until your grandfather confirms Gavin's appointment as his factor. He is only on probation, meantime, didn't you know?"

She walked towards the door.

"Hugh will be getting impatient, wondering what has been keeping us," she said as she turned the handle. "I shall go and tell him that you will be down shortly."

I finished my breakfast and dressed quickly.

Outside, the sun was streaming down from a cloudless sky and the mountain tops of the range on the other side of the loch seemed to shimmer with the misty heat. The water itself reflected the deep blue of the sky as placidly as any mirror, and I knew from past experience that this was going to be one of those incomparable summer days which often follow a day of storms. The kind of day I felt only pleasant things could possibly happen, and one of the pleasant things I had to look forward to was my afternoon's tour of the estate with Gavin.

As I applied a touch of pale pink lipstick to my smiling mouth, I decided that if Gavin was as interested in Lois as Phyllis and even Rory seemed to think, he would not have arranged to take me out with him this afternoon. It was quite possible that he was tiring of her, as he had tired of so many girls in the past, after a brief, passionate flirtation, and my presence at Tarris was giving him an excuse to wangle out of a possible entanglement.

With this hopeful thought in mind, I ran lightly downstairs to my grandfather's room. I sat and chatted happily with him for about half an hour. Then, when I saw that he seemed to be tiring a little, I decided it was time for me to take my leave. I stood up to go, but he held out a detaining hand.

"Before you leave me, Joanna," he said with a note of gravity in his voice, "I should like to discuss your future with you."

"My future?" I raised my brows in surprise.

"Yes. I have had this on my mind for some time." His hands plucked thoughtfully at the bedcover.

"As you know you are my only grandchild, and Tarris is an old estate, which the Conynghame family has had for many generations."

He sighed. "If my only son had not been killed during the war, things would have been different. There could have been a direct male heir to carry on the line." He stopped, and there was a faraway look in his eyes, as if he was remembering his loss, and the might have beens.

"As it is," he continued slowly, "Gavin, my nephew, and the only surviving male member of the family, will inherit my title. I am also gifting him the home farm, to keep his interests bound to Tarrisdale."

He took a deep breath and went on, with the ghost of a smile. "Naturally I have made proper provision for Phyllis, who will be granted the use of the west wing of Tarris for as long as she desires it, over and above the money I have settled on her, and your mother too, since blood is thicker than water, will be well provided for.

"However, the important thing is this. As my one direct grandchild, I am bequeathing you the estate of Tarris, in trust, with an adequate sum for its maintenance. I know you love the place and will see that it is well looked after—"

"Grandfather!" I interrupted, but he held up a hand to command my silence.

"Finally, should you be unmarried, or have no children at the time of your death, Tarris will go to Gavin, and the money in trust will be divided equally between him and Rory, whom I regard as one of the family. However, it is only right that since Gavin is a Conynghame, he should be the one to have Tarris in these circumstances."

I shivered.

"Grandpa!" I protested. "I wish you would not go on about deaths and dying! It gives me the creeps!"

"My dear," he shook his head. "I am not being morbid, merely sensible, in making these arrangements. I thought everything out very carefully before making my will. I am getting on in years, and a man of my age who does not wisely see to the disposition of his possessions, especially when these possessions are such as mine, is wanting in sense. I have seen too much squabbling over property and inheritances to want the same thing to happen here."

I sighed. "I suppose you are right," I admitted. "Yet I don't feel I deserve Tarris, much as I love it."

"But you will look after it, won't you, my dear? This has always been a happy estate, and the personal touch means a lot."

I went to the window and looked out across the sunny garden, and the dark green hedges of rhododendrons with their fading purple blooms which from this particular window cut off the spectacular view of Loch Tarris and the harbour of Tarrisdale.

"Supposing," I mused, "supposing I marry, and my husband's job means that we could not live here, what then?"

He looked thoughtful. "There is always that, of course. Still, Gavin is making a good job of managing the estate at the moment—a surprisingly good job—" Grandfather nodded his head. "If you could not live at Tarris yourself, possibly you could come to some arrangement with him about looking after it for you."

He drew a deep breath. "One of my dreams was to see your children here, at Tarris, Joanna."

"In that case," I said lightly. "Perhaps I should marry Gavin. That would be the ideal answer!"

The shrewd old eyes studied my face.

"As I understand it from Morag, Gavin is as good as engaged to old Burgess's pretty daughter, isn't that right?"

"I was being facetious!" I said quickly.

"Were you, my dear?" he inquired knowingly. "Or were you indulging in a day dream? I remember how fond you used to be of Gavin, always trailing after him, and at one time I had hopes that you and he—" His voice trailed off in a sigh. "Things never work out as we plan them, do they?"

Before I could reply, Phyllis came into the room carrying a vase filled with newly cut roses.

"This has been a wonderful summer for blooms," she said as she placed the vase on a table by the window. "I think I shall order some more rose bushes to put round the summer house."

"If you had your way, Phyllis, you would grow roses and not seedling pines in our plantations!" teased grandfather, smiling fondly at her.

"I noticed a big difference in the garden," I remarked. "It is much gayer than it used to be. I remember mother wanted to make a rose plot in front of the house, but she didn't like suggesting it to grandpa. I believe she was a little bit afraid of you!" I turned to him.

"Your mother was never afraid of anything in her life!" he contradicted me.

"She was when it came to making alterations in the house. She thought you might like to keep things as they had been when grandmother was alive, and she did not want to offend you by pointing out that even furniture can wear out, and fashions in furnishings change!"

"I felt like that myself when I came here first of all!" Phyllis agreed with me, "but gradually I got round to doing the things I wanted to do. After all," she went on slowly, "as my husband kept telling me, this was my home now, and I was to make it into the kind of home I would be happy in."

She plumped up the pillows behind my grandfather.

"By the way, Rory is going down to the village in a few minutes, Hugh. Is there anything you would like him to get for you?" she asked.

"Do you think he would mind changing the library books for me again? He knows the kind of thing I enjoy reading."

He turned to me.

"You go down with him, Joanna. It will give you something to do. The books to be returned are over there, on the dressing table."

Chapter Ten

Rory was tinkering round under the bonnet of his car when I went outside carrying the library books.

He looked up when he heard my footsteps on the forecourt, and grinned when he saw what I was bringing him.

"Not again!" he shook his head. "Your grandfather has read every book in the local library at least twice since I came on holiday. I know it is all he has to pass the time because he is not very keen on watching television, but there is not a very big selection of books for me to choose from in Tarrisdale."

"He seemed to think you would know what to get for him."

"I know his tastes all right," shrugged Rory. "War stories, adventure stories, thrillers, anything with plenty of action in it amuses him, but I doubt if even he could be bothered to read the same thing for a third time!"

He banged down the bonnet and opened the car door for me to get in, at the same time glancing at his watch.

"If you don't mind being driven at speed, we could get to Fort William and back before lunch," he suggested. "We might be able to pick up some new paperbacks for him in one of the shops there. How about it?" he asked as he slipped behind the driving seat.

"You are sure we shall be back in time for lunch?" I demanded anxiously as we started off down the driveway. I did not want to be late for my looked forward to appointment with Gavin in the afternoon.

"We shall have to be," he said positively. "I haven't told Phyllis we are going to Fort William and she would worry if we weren't back by lunchtime."

He changed gear for the sharp hairpin corner we were coming to, took it at a reasonable speed, then accelerated to nip past a farm tractor which was ambling slowly down the hill, and slowed again for the right angled turn into the High Street. A few minutes later we stopped outside the little County Library and Rory went in to carry out his commission.

As I sat waiting for him in his car, Lois Burgess drove past in Gavin's Jaguar, and drew up in front of the Lotus. She got out of the car, and with a barely perceptible smile in my direction, strolled into the library.

I followed her with my eyes. She and Gavin must be on fairly intimate terms if he allowed her to use his car about as much as he did himself. I frowned. Perhaps after all there was something to what Phyllis had hinted about a pending engagement. This afternoon, I determined to find out exactly what the situation was.

If nothing had been settled between Lois and Gavin, all being fair in love and war, I saw no reason why I should not resume an old friendship, and with our sharing of so many mutual interests, encourage Gavin to notice me not merely as someone he had been used to seeing about the place, but as a personality in my own right, someone attractive enough to make him forget his infatuation for Lois Burgess; someone with whom he could fall genuinely in love.

What a fairy tale ending that would be I thought blissfully. Not only would my own adolescent dream come true, but grandfather's too, for Tarris would be kept in the family in a most satisfactory way.

I smiled to myself at the idea, and Rory, walking across from the library to join me, eyed me curiously and said:

"It's nice to see someone looking cheerful! Poor Lois is not in the best of moods. Her father is not too well today, so she has to spend her afternoon showing a client from Glasgow over Heather Lodge."

He started the car.

"I expect her father is lucky to have a client interest in the Lodge," I remarked. "I don't suppose there is much demand for houses in Tarrisdale."

I settled comfortably back into my seat and watched the wonderful variety of constantly changing colours in the passing scene as we climbed up the steep road from the village to the pass which led out of it, the road which only yesterday, although already it seemed days ago, I had been transported down in the ambulance.

"Oddly enough, there is," said Rory. "Now that the modern wonders of electricity, television and fast road transport have reached this part of the world, more and more people are looking for houses here in which to spend their retirement."

"In that case, as the only lawyer in the district, Burgess must do quite well?"

Rory nodded. "From what I hear, he does, but he would need to, with a daughter like Lois. She spends money like water, and has the most extravagant ideas. Phyllis had to be very firm about some of the furnishings she wanted to order when Tarris was being redecorated."

I gave a shudder, and averted my eyes from the gash marks along the face of the cliff and the fragments of glass swept into the side of the road, which marked the spot where I had had my brush with death the previous day and there was a dry lump in my throat as I replied, quickly trying to take my mind from the shocked realization of how lucky I had been.

"She will have to cut down a lot if she marries Gavin. He is not in the millionaire bracket, or anything like it!"

I gave him a sideways look. "Do you really think they are serious about each other?"

Rory shrugged. "I am only going by what I have heard from Phyllis, and what she, in turn, heard from Morag, who seems to think Lois will make Gavin a suitable wife, and believes he is merely waiting until he has satisfied your grandfather about his competence to run Tarris permanently, before he asks her to marry him." He looked straight ahead as he added, "Marriage will have a settling influence on them both."

"You make marriage sound dull!" I exclaimed. "Almost as if it is a business proposition!"

He shot me an amused glance. "I suppose you believe in love at first sight, and happy ever after, with never a thought that day to day living can be very prosaic?"

"Yes, I do!" I said defiantly. "And I wouldn't let my marriage become dull and pedestrian!"

Rory laughed. "That's a refreshing change from some of the ideas I have heard expounded about wedded bliss these past years. I hope you will never be disillusioned, Joanna!"

"That is up to me, isn't it? And I would make my marriage a happy one," I said determinedly.

"Bully for you!" Rory's voice was gently mocking.

I ignored the mockery, and turned my attention once more to the passing scene.

On my left, Loch Linnhe sparkled like silver plate in the sunshine, and a couple of fishing boats, their gleaming black hulls reflecting back the glitter of the wavelets, sailed down towards the Firth of Lorne.

The mountainsides were jacketed with the rich, deep green of pine and lighter green of larch, and the smell of seaweed from the pebbly shore of the loch, mingled with the sweet smell of the trailing honeysuckle and the white marguerites by the roadside was fragrant and satisfying, and no doubt much more aromatic than the smell of Venice's Grand Canal would have been.

Patches of mountain thyme made vivid splashes of lilac pink on the rocky outcrops, and bushes of late flowering broom formed a golden haze to cover the rock scars where the hillside had been blasted away to make the broad, new roadway.

The mountains gradually receded from the road to give way to gently sloping meadows for sheep and cattle, and the fences which hopefully kept the flocks from straying across the roadway were decked with the lavender trumpets of wild convolvulous and the deep purple of climbing vetches.

Farmland gave way to the first few straggling houses on the outskirts of Fort William, and modern bungalows in neatly landscaped gardens contrasted with the older grey sandstone houses which seemed to huddle for protection against the winter storms behind thick hedges of laurel and rhododendron.

Being the height of summer, Fort William was busy. Its narrow streets were jammed with traffic and noisy, not only with the sound of harsh gear changing and revving engines and admonitory klaxons, but also with the cheerful chatter of the many tourists from the world over, to whom the town is a gateway to Scotland's magnificent North West scenery.

Rory managed to squeeze the Lotus into a parking place near the pier, and we stood for a few minutes to watch the Island ferry sail away.

"I think there is something exciting about ports and railway stations and airports, don't you?" I turned, smiling to my companion. "I always get an irresistible urge to board the boat or train or airliner which is about to leave, and be transported to another city, another country, or even," I braved his mockery, "even another world, when the space programme gets into its stride.

"You are a born romantic and a born adventurer, it seems, Joanna," he looked at me with amusement in his eyes. "Travel can have its boring side too, you know!"

"Do you think so? I love travelling—meeting new people, seeing new countrysides, learning other customs, eating strange foods and absorbing other cultures. That was why I was looking forward so much to my trip to Venice. It is a city, and a civilization, which has always attracted me."

"So you are sorry to be here now, rather than in Italy?" he challenged. "I am sorry if I spoiled your plans."

"You haven't spoilt anything," I assured him. "I am so glad you had the sense to send for me, and as for Venice, well, there is always tomorrow."

I laughed. "Do you know, that is what my mother used to say when we came to shop in Fort William and I asked her if we could spend the day climbing Ben Nevis instead."

I glanced round in the direction of Britain's highest mountain. "That is one ambition I have never realized."

"You are staying at Tarris for the rest of your holiday, aren't you?" asked Rory.

"Of course!"

"Then in that case, you could realize your ambition. We could climb it together, if you like."

"Rory! Do you mean that?" I turned to look at him, my eyes shining with pleasure. "That would be wonderful! You can't imagine how much I shall look forward to that!"

I smiled up at him, and as he smiled down at me I had the oddest sensation, almost like an electric shock, which sent little quivers of excitement feathering up and down my spine.

"I hope you have a good, stout pair of walking shoes," Rory's matter of fact pronouncement broke the spell. "Or is the rest of your footwear on a par with those pretty, but senseless golden sandals you were wearing last night?"

"You need not worry on that score. Even sight-seeing in Italy demands sturdy and comfortable shoes," I enlightened him. "I learned that from experience!"

"Good!" he commended me, as he put his hand on my arm to propel me safely across the busy thoroughfare, and once again I felt that inexplicable shiver of excitement.

We insinuated our way past the dawdling tourists on the narrow pavements, until we reached a newsagent's shop, where we were able to buy a very good selection of paperbacks for grandfather's delectation.

I also bought a tartan travelling rug for my mother, in the Fraser tartan, and when we were passing a women's dress shop, I spotted a navy and silk head square, with a lovely moss pink rose design, and impulsively I went in to buy it for Phyllis.

Rory waited impatiently outside the shop, and when I came out with my parcel, he told me sharply that we had not come to Fort William on a shopping spree.

As it was, we would be hard pushed to get back to Tarrisdale for one o'clock lunch.

Chapter Eleven

Grandfather was delighted when Rory and I went to his room and handed him the miscellany of paperbacks we had bought for him.

"How good of you to go to all this trouble for me!" he smiled gratefully. "These books should keep me occupied for some time! What do you think, Phyllis?" he turned to his wife.

"I can see I am not going to get a word out of you for days!" she agreed, arranging the books on the table beside his bed.

When she had done so, I said to her, shyly presenting her with the small gift I had bought in Fort William:

"This is for you, Phyllis."

She looked puzzled. "For me?"

Rory gave me an equally puzzled look, because I had not told him what I had been buying.

"It is just a little thing which I saw in one of the shops this morning," I explained. "I thought you might like it."

"What is it?" She felt the parcel tentatively.

"You will find that out when you unwrap it, my dear!" Grandfather was as curious about the packet as the other two.

Phyllis stripped away the gummed tape and tore off the wrapping paper. More slowly she removed the tissue paper.

"My dear Joanna!" she exclaimed with genuine pleasure when she saw the contents. "How lovely! Hugh! Look at this!"

She held up the scarf for her husband's inspection. "What a nice grand-daughter you have!"

Impulsively she came over and gave me a warm hug.

"Thank you very, very much, Joanna. You could not have chosen a more acceptable gift."

My cheeks reddened with embarrassment, and I mumbled like an adolescent schoolgirl that I was glad she liked it.

To my relief, Mrs Oliver knocked on the door at this moment, and came in carrying grandfather's luncheon tray, and informed us that our own meal was ready.

"There was a telephone call for you, Mr Armstrong," she went on, addressing Rory. "From Miss Henderson. She asked if you would get in touch with her."

"You can call her after lunch," said Phyllis. "This is cook's half day, and she likes to get away as early as possible so as not to miss the bus to the village."

"I am going to Tarrisdale myself after lunch," replied Rory. "I can give Mrs Love a lift if she likes. At least," he frowned, "I was going to Tarrisdale, because I had promised to go sailing with Sally, but of course something may have cropped up to prevent her keeping our date."

"You will find out about that once you telephone her," said Phyllis leading the way into the dining-room.

We ate our meal quickly and in silence, each of us immersed in our own thoughts. I was thinking so much about the afternoon ahead, when I would have Gavin to myself, that I scarcely heard Rory ask to be excused to go and make his call.

It was not until Phyllis remarked that since Dr Menzies was bringing one of his specialist friends to visit grandfather that afternoon, and that she would need time to tidy his bedroom before their arrival, that I came out of my reverie.

"I hope you will be able to entertain yourself, Joanna," she went on. "I am sorry that Rory had this previous engagement, or you could have gone sailing with him."

"Oh! Didn't I tell you? Gavin is calling for me this afternoon. He wants to take me round Tarris to show me the changes that have taken place since I was here last, and to tell me about the new developments he has in hand. He knows how interested I have always been in what is happening on the estate, and that I shall be equally interested in the new schemes."

"I am sure you will, Joanna. Gavin has some very forward looking ideas, in more ways than one," she added dryly. "I do not know if he has already told you that he wants to make Tarris a show place to demonstrate what could be done to other estates in the Highlands."

I shook my head and she went on:

"He also talks of damming one of the mountain streams at the northern extremity of the estate, to make a small, artificial loch, and stock it with trout, and lease the fishing rights, and of draining the flat fields near Invertarris and growing bulbs there for export!"

"Good heavens!" I exclaimed. "As you say, Gavin is certainly very forward looking. He must have put a lot of thought into the future of Tarris."

"It could be his own future too," said Phyllis slowly. "I have no doubt that it is because of these proposed innovations he wants to take you around, to study your reactions to them. After all," she went on, and there was a hint of sadness in her voice, "we all know that you will inherit Tarris one day, Joanna, and Gavin will want to impress you with his capabilities so that in the event of anything happening to Hugh, you will keep him on in his present job as manager of the estate."

Her expressive face clouded. "These last attacks have left Hugh very weak, and I live in constant dread of another attack, when he is lacking the stamina to fight it."

"But surely if grandfather has rest and quiet and no unnecessary excitement, there is no reason why he should not gain strength?" I tried to cheer her. "And it must be a great weight off his shoulders to have Gavin take over the work of the estate so competently?"

She gave me a grateful smile.

"It is nice to have someone like you to talk to, Joanna. I cannot discuss my concern for Hugh with the staff, or my social acquaintances." Her smile saddened. "You know Tarrisdale. Although I have lived here for five years now, and play the part expected of me in the village life, I am still looked on as an incomer. Gavin's mother is inclined to resent me, although she does her best not to show it. Lois is Lois and concerned only with her own interests, and although young Sally is a dear, she has enough to worry about with an invalid mother to look after. Of course, there is Rory, but he is not here all the time, and in any case, men see things from a different point of view."

"Rory likes Sally, doesn't he?"

"Rory has an eye for a pretty girl, and when he comes here, he and Sally sometimes go out together," she replied non-committally.

I was on the point of asking her what Rory did, but as we were leaving the room, we could hear the tinkle as grandfather's little handbell was shaken vigorously, and Phyllis excused herself and went hurrying off to see what her husband wanted.

I went upstairs to freshen up and put on my walking shoes for the afternoon tour of the estate, and then went out to sit in the sun on the low wall which divided the flagged courtyard from the rose garden, and await Gavin's arrival.

Rory emerged from the house a minute or two later, accompanied by the cook, an enormously fat and cheerful-looking woman whom I vaguely remembered as being the widow of a local fisherman.

Rory opened the passenger door of his Lotus

and tried to help her into the car. It was a tight squeeze, and as she sat down, the car sagged almost to the ground.

Rory saw me watching the proceedings, and he flashed me an amused grin. I grinned back, because, considering how difficult it had been to get his passenger into the car, I could well imagine the fun he was going to have, trying to get her out of it when they reached the village!

Rory slipped in behind the driving wheel, gave me a gay wave of farewell, and at a very sedate pace, more for consideration of his car's springs than for his passenger, I thought, he started off down the drive, and I watched the yellow Lotus until it was out of sight.

Gavin arrived in the estate Land Rover not long after and drew up alongside where I was sitting.

"Hello, Joanna!" he greeted me with a cheerful smile. "I hope I haven't kept you waiting too long."

"I was enjoying the sunshine," I replied as he gave me a hand to pull me up into the Land Rover.

"You will see the place at its very best," he nodded. "There is so much I want to show you!" he went on enthusiastically.

As we drove along the road and turned east into a narrow forestry track, deeply rutted by the wheels of tractors and heavy lorries, I glanced at my companion.

The open air life he was leading had tanned his cheeks and bleached his fair hair almost white, and with his splendid Conynghame features and the clear Conynghame blue eyes, he made me think of a Norse god. It was small wonder that I had made an idol of him in the past, and that every girl in the district had been equally infatuated.

Gavin turned round suddenly and caught me looking at him.

He grinned. "This is just like old times, isn't it? Remember how you always used to tag along with Uncle Hugh and me when we did our rounds of the estate? I used to think how unusual it was for a girl of your age to be so interested in the management of the place."

I laughed. "Come off it, Gavin! Tell the truth and say that in those days you barely even noticed me! You and grandfather were too busy discussing things like drainage and the merits of certain grasses for grazing, and the restocking of the river, and the bracken curse, to pay any attention to me!"

"Touché!" he admitted with a smile. "All the same, I don't know why I didn't pay you more attention, or were you not as pretty in those days as you are now?"

"Now you are trying to talk your way out!" I teased.

He laughed. "Perhaps the truth is, even in those days, I could not see beyond Tarris. It was my first love. I remember when I was away at boarding school, dreaming of the days when I would be back here, fishing in the streams, exploring the woods and helping the shepherd with his sheep on the upper pastures. I suppose you could say I was obsessed by the place."

He stopped the Land Rover in a clearing and jumped down.

"We shall walk from here," he said and came round to help me. He swung me easily to the ground, and held me firmly round the waist, until I was properly balanced on my feet. For that second I could feel the steady beat of his heart against mine, and for a moment longer than was really necessary he held me tight, before pushing me away, smiling, and said lightly:

"Come on, Joanna. We haven't all day to waste."

I strode behind him along a narrow track through the trees, avoiding trailing bramble bushes and exposed tree roots and damp, muddy puddles which formed natural hazards on our way.

The track petered out some hundred feet farther on, at the edge of a broad, marshy field, where rushes grew in profusion and here and there a marsh andromeda, or a splash of gold from globe flower blossoms, or the lavender spears of the spotted orchis broke the monotony of the reed green.

"Do you see this area, Joanna?" Gavin made a broad sweep with his hand. "One day I hope to drain it, and grow spring bulbs here. It is sheltered by the mountains from all but the west wind, and the ground is rich and peaty." He bent down and picked up a lump of earth which he crumbled between his fingers.

"They have experimented successfully with growing bulbs on some of the islands, so why not here, where transport would not be such a problem?"

He dropped the remaining peat to the ground.

"I am waiting for your grandfather to give the go ahead to this scheme. He still seems a bit dubious."

"I think it is a wonderful idea," I said enthusiastically. "I would rather see fields of daffodils than marshland any day! But what about the cost of drainage? And the initial cost of planting? And transport? You would need a better road than that track we have just come along."

"So it is not only a pretty face you have, Joanna!" he looked at me with growing respect.

"That is just my training coming out," I told him. "I can see the makings of an interesting article in the work you are planning here, and an article is no good unless it is full of facts, which are both accurate and exciting."

"So between us we could put Tarris on the map!" Gavin looked thoughtful. "You with your writing about the place, and me with my schemes. We must talk over this one evening, but meantime, come and see some of my other projects."

The afternoon passed all too quickly. I was as fascinated at what could be done to improve the estate as Gavin was, and deeply impressed by the amount of thought he had put into his ideas to make Tarris a place of importance.

Gavin seemed to know every yard of the land and its potential. What was more, he knew all the workers on it by name, and seemed to command their respect. This day I saw a very different Gavin to the image I had had of him as a gay, romantic, devil-may-care young man, and I was surprised at the intensity of his love for Tarris.

I wondered if Lois shared his enthusiasm, or if they had other things in common.

"Do you still race at Ingleston, Gavin?" I asked curiously when we were on our way home. "I remember how wonderful I thought you were, winning a race there once!"

"I raced occasionally after that," he spoke slowly, "but it is an expensive business, and since my father died, I have not had that kind of money. Why do all the things one wants have to be so expensive?" he ended with a sigh.

"Like Lois?" I asked slyly.

His hand tightened on the driving wheel, and a guarded look made his face lose all expression.

He deliberately misunderstood me, and said in reply:

"Yes, Lois likes the good things in life too, but don't we all?"

"Some more than others," I still probed.

"I daresay, and sometimes when we find out what it is we do want, we have to hurt others to get it. I don't like hurting people, Joanna, but sometimes it has to be done."

I shivered slightly. There was a tightness now

about Gavin's mouth, and I wondered what he was thinking about, and who he was afraid would be hurt before he got what he wanted.

Chapter Twelve

When we arrived back at Tarris House, Phyllis was in the rose garden, cutting off the dead flower heads. She came forward to meet me as I jumped down from the Land Rover.

"Did you enjoy your afternoon, Joanna?" she asked as she peeled off her tough gardening gloves and laid them in the trug beside the secateurs.

"Very much!" I told her. "I still can hardly take in all the changes that have taken place since the last time I was here."

"Hugh admits that Gavin has put forward some very interesting proposals for development, but he is still not very sure if they should be put into practice or not. He will no doubt be interested in your opinion."

"How can you know if something will succeed unless you try it?" Gavin joined in the discussion. "How is Uncle Hugh this afternoon? Well enough for me to have a word with him?"

"He seems very much better, and Dr Menzies is very pleased with the improvement in him, and says he can now get up for an hour or two each afternoon!" Phyllis said happily.

"I am glad to hear that. I hope he won't overdo things."

"I think he has learnt his lesson this time, Gavin. I hope so! You can go in and have a word with him now, but don't be too long, and don't say anything to worry him. Mrs Oliver is serving afternoon tea in about ten minutes, so I shall tell her to add an extra cup. We shall be in the morning-room," she added.

Gavin strolled towards the house and I followed Phyllis to the garden shed behind the rose plots.

"I thought Rory would have been back by this time," she cast a frowning glance down the drive. "He had to cancel his arrangement to go sailing with Sally because something else cropped up, something to do with our famous local fête next week. Like myself, Sally is on the committee, and like Gavin she is always full of bright new ideas how things should be done. She has even managed to rope Rory in to lending a helping hand with one of the stalls, which is more than I could do!"

"I remember those Fêtes!" I laughed. "They were the highlight of the summer season here in Tarrisdale! Does Mrs Halliday still do the fortune telling with her gypsy costume and crystal ball? I never missed a chance of paying over my money to find out what fate had in store for me!"

Phyllis looked amused.

"How many tall, dark and handsome men have crossed your path since those days?" she teased gently.

"Dozens!" I replied lightly.

"I wonder what Lois will predict for you when you go to the fortune-teller's tent this year?" she asked with a twinkle in her eye. "I don't think that it will be a blue-eyed Aryan type somehow!"

"Don't tell me that Lois has taken over from Mrs Halliday!" I looked at her with disbelief.

"No one else was willing to follow in the old lady's footsteps, but Gavin managed to talk Lois into giving it a try. I should not be at all surprised if she made a success of it. It is the kind of thing I think will appeal to her. She is a bit of an actress, don't you agree?"

"She certainly likes holding the centre of the stage!" I sniffed cattily.

Phyllis's eyes smiled, but she managed to keep her mouth straight as she replied mildly.

"Joanna, my dear," her tone was cautionary. "Your prejudice is showing!"

"She just isn't my type," I shrugged and followed Phyllis back to the house.

We were entering the front door when the subject of our discussion came racing up the drive in the Jaguar, followed at a more sedate pace by Rory and Sally in the yellow Lotus.

"I told you mine was the better car!" she called triumphantly to Rory as she stepped out of her vehicle. Seeing us she called to explain. "We had a race from the village."

Rory said nothing as he alighted from his car, but the expression on his face was far from amused, which surprised me, because I had not expected him to be a poor loser.

Lois, ignoring his dark looks strolled across to us, looking very elegant in a sleeveless fine wool dress of brilliant orange, and went on, a touch of impatience in her voice:

"Where is Gavin? He said he would be here."

"Gavin is talking business with his uncle," said Phyllis smoothly, "and since he is also going to join us for afternoon tea, perhaps you will too? Joanna," she turned to me with a smile, "be a dear and tell Mrs Oliver there is another extra guest."

I went ahead of the party into the house, to seek out Mrs Oliver in the kitchen, where I gave her a hand to butter some extra scones and cut some more slabs of fresh, fruity Dundee cake. By the time we were ready, Gavin had joined the others in the morning-room.

I helped Phyllis serve the tea, and as I handed round the cups, Sally said to me:

"Remember we were talking about Holy Willie last night? Well, the police did go to see him, which was just as well for him, because they found him huddled unconscious in a corner of his shack."

"What was wrong with him?" asked Gavin.

"Apparently he collapsed two days ago with dreadful pains in his stomach, and was too weak even to crawl to the door to try to attract Molly Mackay's attention."

"They took him to the hospital, and he recovered sufficiently to answer their questions. However, he was not able to be of any help to them."

"Poor old Willie!" said Gavin. "But it is an ill

wind. Now that the authorities have got him into hospital, they should be able to keep him there, in their geriatric ward, and we shall be able to get rid of his old shack for good. It has been an insanitary eyesore to the community for far too long."

"However unsightly the shack is, surely you cannot destroy a man's home when he isn't there to do anything about it!" I was appalled.

"My dear girl! It is for his own good!" protested Gavin. "If he has nowhere to go, he will be only too pleased to stay on in hospital, where he can be taken care of."

"It may be for his own good in one way," I snapped, "but how would you like it if someone took over your home and your possessions when your back was turned, and destroyed them?"

Sally sprang to Gavin's defence.

"Joanna! You haven't seen that shack recently. It is in a dreadful condition. Actually the Sanitary Department was going to do something about it at their next meeting. This makes it easy for them to go ahead with their plans."

"But what about his personal possessions?" I persisted. "We all have little bits and pieces which are precious to us, although others may not be aware of their value."

"All his personal possessions will be carefully packed up and kept in store for him," Sally assured me. "I am going down to the shack on Monday with Dr Menzies and one of the policemen to go over his things and see what is worth salvaging."

"Poor old Willie!" I said sadly. "This is the end of a legend. He will not be the same character after he has been hospitalized."

"He will be a much cleaner one!" said Lois with a sniff. "The authorities should have taken a firmer hand with him years ago, and had him put away."

Rather than provoke further argument, I said no more, and Phyllis tactfully changed the subject by saying:

"Is that all your news, Sally?"

Sally shook her head. "No, as a matter of fact! Someone pinched Dr Menzies' car for a joyride last night. He had left it outside his gate as usual, but it wasn't there when he went for it this morning. Later, the police found it abandoned among some trees in lower Tarris Wood."

"Who on earth would do a mean thing like that?"

"The police think it was taken by the tinker lads who are camping further up the glen," said Rory, "but naturally they all deny having anything to do with it."

"Naturally!" commented Gavin dryly.

"I wonder if it was the same person or persons who pinched the lorry?" I conjectured.

"At least they did not wreck the doctor's car!" said Sally. "And they did not mess it about inside either, although it was filthy outside, almost as if they had been driving through fields or along the forestry tracks."

"Young devils!" growled Gavin. "If they want to work out their energy on something, I could give them plenty to do that would keep them out of further mischief!"

"Talking of giving people something to do reminds me." Sally looked at me. "Joanna, would you like to take charge of the "Ring the Bottle" at the Garden Fête? Harry Brown, who was to have done so, has had to go south on business, and I cannot think of anyone else who would not be offended at being asked at the last minute."

"People might be more offended if I took over the job," I demurred. "After all, it is a local show, and I have been away from Tarrisdale for so long, that it might be out of place for me to take an active part in it."

"Nonsense!" said Sally. "If it was not for the support the Conynghames give them, the Fête would not be half the success it has been. In any case," she added with a twinkle, "think what an attraction it will be having you at one of the stalls. People will come to try to "Ring the Bottle" out of curiosity to see what you look like after being away from here for five years!"

"You make me sound like a circus freak!" I giggled.

"Of course you must come!" said Lois decisively. "We are all doing something at the Fête. Even Gavin is taking a day off to help organize the treasure hunt."

"And you will be right next to me!" cajoled Rory. "I am in charge of the shooting range."

"That is enough to put me off!" I joked. "The last Fête I attended, Mike Hallam decided he could hit the bull's eye by looking in a mirror and firing over his shoulder. Instead of hitting the target, he killed the goose that was being auctioned in the next stall!"

"I remember that!" said Gavin. "There was quite a fuss about it, and there was even talk of having no shooting range at the next Fête."

"They black-balled Mike instead!" said Sally. "The shooting is too big an attraction to do away with."

We spent the next half hour discussing the Fête until Lois decided it was time to go home.

"Do you want a lift, Sally?" she asked. "It will save Rory going out again if I take you."

Sally hesitated for the fraction of a second, and seeing her hesitation, Rory said quickly:

"I have to go down to Tarrisdale in any case, Lois, and Sally's house is off your road."

Lois shrugged and said, "In that case, I shall get on my way. Oh, Gavin," she turned to my cousin, "shall I leave your car at your house, or will you come and collect it from mine?"

"You can bring it along tonight when you come to see mother about the new curtains for the lounge," he replied. "She is expecting you to call about eight o'clock, she told me."

He followed her from the room, and Sally looked at Rory and said gratefully:

"Thanks for letting me off the hook, Rory. Lois's style of driving terrifies me."

"It terrifies me too," agreed Rory. "I am surprised she has never been involved in a serious accident, and I am more than surprised that Gavin trusts his car to her."

"Gavin is soft-hearted, that is his trouble," said Sally. "I think he feels sorry for Lois. You know what a bad deal she had with that firm in London. It made her lose confidence in herself, and Gavin is trying to boost her morale."

"Gavin never gave a damn for anyone's morale!" I shook my head, remembering how he had teased me in adolescence. "And I very much doubt if Lois's confidence in herself could ever be undermined."

"You are wrong about Gavin," said Sally firmly. "He would never hurt anyone intentionally, I'm sure."

She seemed determined to look for the best in everyone and I had to admire her for this. Possibly it was her kind nature which appealed to Rory. My eyes flickered in his direction speculatively, and yet I would have thought that he was a man who preferred spice to sweetness.

"I shall bring my car round from the garage," he said. "I shan't be long. Do you want to come with us?" he asked me.

"Hugh wants to have a word with Joanna about the estate. He is eager to hear what she thinks about Gavin's ideas."

I felt a momentary flicker of annoyance at being done out of my trip with Rory, which was inexplicable in view of the fact that usually I dislike making up a threesome.

As I helped Phyllis replace the cups and

plates on the tea trolley, prior to going in to see my grandfather, I kept wondering why I should have felt that spasm of resentment against her for stopping me going off with the other two.

Chapter Thirteen

I went to bed early that evening, and in the comfort of the turquoise guest-room the odd creaks and groans, the mournful sighing of the wind in the chimney, and the distant cry of a marauding owl did not affect me as they had done on the previous night in my remote and lonely bedroom in the west wing.

The following day, being Sunday, I knew that the household would not be astir as early as usual, and I lay on, in sleepy contentment at the thought of being home again, until I heard the sound of other movements in the house, and then I got up and joined Phyllis and her son for nine o'clock breakfast.

Grandfather had had a good night's rest, and was already engrossed in one of the thrillers Rory and I had bought him the previous day.

Phyllis was of the opinion that he was now well enough to be left in the care of Mrs Oliver, and following the family tradition, she decided that we should go the the morning service in the Parish church.

We left grandfather sitting propped up comfortably in his bed, with his books to hand, and the bell with which he could summon Mrs Oliver under his pillow. His favourite cat, a sleek, amber-eyed tabby, elected to keep him company, and curled itself into a comfortable position at the foot of his bed, where it purred contentedly as we took our leave.

Gavin and his mother joined us in the family pew, and Sally Henderson, very young and demure looking in a navy costume with white lapels and a white straw boater, led the soprano section of the choir.

I noticed her looking across at our pew from time to time, and I wondered if Rory was fully aware of the way Sally felt about him, or if he merely regarded her as one more attractive female to dally with when he was on holiday.

During the sermon I found my attention wandering. In front of me, the bank manager's head had slumped forward, and his wife gave him a sharp nudge to waken him up. Old Mrs Lewis, still sporting the grey flannel coat and the black straw hat generously trimmed with outsize cherries which she had worn for summer services for as long as I could remember, surreptitiously sucked a sweetmeat, whose strong peppermint smell must have been noticeable even in the pulpit, and Phyllis was gazing absorbed at the play of sunlight through the richly coloured stain glass of the War Memorial window to the left of the choir.

From her engrossed expression my eyes passed to the faces of the two men seated between her and my Aunt Morag. There could not have been a greater contrast as far as looks were concerned, with Gavin so blond and sharp featured and slim built, and Rory so dark and craggy faced and, because of his breadth of shoulder, looking more squarely built than the other man, although they were much the same height.

Gavin's left fingers were beating an impatient rhythm on his knees, as if he wanted the sermon to be over and done with, so that he could get about his own business.

I smiled. Gavin had always been an impatient being, inclined to tackle a fresh job before the one in hand was finished; inclined to leave someone else to do his tidying up for him, for that matter.

Perhaps that was why grandfather was not too keen about his grandiose schemes for Tarris; perhaps he thought Gavin might lose interest there too, but he would have been wrong, I realized. In some things, like his gay flirtations, Gavin might blow hot and cold quickly, but his feeling for Tarris was very deep, a genuine passion, as I had learned yesterday, and Tarris would never be neglected by him, although he might neglect other things for Tarris.

I wondered how Lois would enjoy playing second fiddle to the estate, and this thought made me stir uneasily in my seat.

At my movement, Rory turned and glanced in my direction. A shaft of sunlight reflected on to his face from the shining brass of the eagle on the lectern, and emphasized the black bushiness of his brows and seemed to elongate his features, giving him an almost satanic look, which was dispelled the moment his mouth softened in a smile as he realized I was watching him.

I quickly dropped my eyes and pretended to be engaged in turning the pages of the hymn book to look for the final hymn, but although I was no longer looking at him, I was aware that he continued to look at me, and for some reason, I grew tense under his scrutiny, and could not control a faint blush from staining my cheeks.

I was annoyed with myself for letting Rory's casual interest in me affect me in this way, and I sat rigidly back against the wooden settee so that Phyllis's broad-brimmed hat effectively screened me from his view.

I tried to concentrate on what the minister was saying, but I could not follow his argument because of my previous inattention. I tried to make up for my heedlessness to the sermon by singing the closing hymn with more than usual gusto, which made Mrs Lewis peer round at me and nod her head in approval, to Phyllis's amusement.

When we left the church the minister was standing at the front entrance, waiting to have a word with me and welcome me back once more to Tarrisdale. He then went on to ask Phyllis when it would be convenient for him to call and visit Sir Hugh, and at this point Gavin and his mother made their excuses and left us, and from the corner of my eye, as Phyllis continued to chat to the minister, I saw Gavin stop to speak to Sally, who, after a moment's hesitation, accompanied him to his car, and got in beside his mother.

I felt sorry for Sally. It seemed to me that she had been waiting outside the church not for Gavin, but for Rory to offer to take her home, although, as it happened, she would have been disappointed, because in view of the lovely morning, we had walked from Tarris House the mile and a half down the road to the church, which stands right on the outskirts of the village.

The minister moved off to talk to other members of his congregation, and we were about to set off for home when two of my mother's old friends in the village, the Misses Halbert, came hurrying across to have a word with me.

Phyllis glanced at her watch.

"Joanna, will you excuse me, my dear?" she asked. "I don't like being away from Hugh for any longer than I can help, and I see the bus coming, which will save me the long walk uphill." She fumbled in her handbag for change. "There is no need for you to hurry," she continued. "We always have a very late lunch on Sundays."

I half expected Rory to go with his mother, but he stayed with me, and I was grateful to him for this, because I felt that his presence would inhibit my mother's friends from asking me awkward questions about our relationship with our new family, and prying into the reasons why we had kept away from Tarrisdale for such a number of years.

We chatted to the Halberts for several minutes, until gradually the groups round the church gate thinned out. Then, on the promise that I would visit them before I went south again I managed to get away from the two elderly ladies.

Rory and I strolled homewards at a leisurely pace, neither of us inclined for conversation. Near the gates of Tarris House, Harry Brook, the lorry driver, passed us on his motorbike. I could not help noticing that there was a massive area of discoloration round one of his eyes, and a great strip of plaster across his forehead.

"Harry looks to me as if he has been in the wars," I remarked. "I wonder what he has been up to?"

Rory glanced after him.

"I should not be surprised if Molly Mackay's husband had something to do with it. I heard in the village last night that he was home again, and he wouldn't need to sit long in one of the "locals" before he heard about Brook's lorry being stolen, where it had been stolen from, and why it had been parked where it was."

"Harry Brook should have known better than take up with Molly." I shook my head. "Everyone in the village knows what sort of man Mackay is."

"Perhaps he felt sorry for her."

"Perhaps. On the other hand, from what I can remember of her, Molly is an extremely bonny girl, in a baby doll sort of way. Big blue eyes, pretty hair, and round pink cheeks, but not very bright."

"She certainly could not have been very bright to marry a man like this Mackay is said to be," agreed Rory as we turned in at the gateway and walked along the drive towards the house. "After all, she herself must have had some idea of his character."

"Perhaps she liked being knocked around," I said thoughtfully. "Apparently some people do."

"And some people are born victims," said Rory sombrely.

"Don't say that!" I felt suddenly cold, as if the sun had disappeared behind a cloud. "It's almost as if you were ill wishing her!"

He looked at me in surprise.

"I did not think a girl like you would be superstitious!"

"I am not superstitious!" I defended myself.

He laughed. "Then how do you explain all those visits to the fortune teller's tent at the Fête that Phyllis was telling me about?"

"That was mere schoolgirl romanticism. In any case," I gave a mock sigh, "the right tall, dark and handsome man never showed up!"

"Would that be because the lady prefers blonds?" he challenged me.

I ignored the quip and quickly changed the subject by saying:

"What exactly did you mean when you said "A girl like you" to me? Do tell me, Rory. What kind of girl do you think I am?"

"For one thing, too full of life to be a born victim!" he retorted lightly. "But I think we should leave further discussion of this intriguing subject until another time. I know mother said that lunch was later than usual on a Sunday, but I don't think she meant that we were to take all afternoon to walk back. Do you realize that it is almost two o'clock?"

"Oh, dear!" I exclaimed. "We had better hurry, or cook might threaten to give notice again!"

Chapter Fourteen

The next couple of days passed smoothly. I made a point of sitting with grandfather in the morning while Phyllis spent the time in her studio, putting the finishing touches to the painting she was doing for Lois, and in the afternoons I went down to the village to shop, or chat with old friends, and in the evenings I read, or wandered round the grounds or played tennis with Rory and Gavin, who made a point of calling at Tarris every evening to keep his uncle up to date with what was going on on the estate.

The police were still looking for the person who had stolen Brook's lorry, but to date they had drawn a blank. They still had their suspicions of the young campers in the glen, and were keeping a watchful eye on them in case they planned further mischief. They were also keeping Mackay under surveillance, because he seemed to be spoiling for another fight with Brook, or anyone else who crossed his path.

According to local gossip, Molly had walked out on him, and he had no idea where she had gone, or to whom she had gone. She had not been at their home when he had arrived back on the Saturday night, and when she had not turned up by morning, he had reported her absence to the police.

Of course, even had they wanted to, there was nothing they could do to help him. Molly was of age, and free to go where she pleased, and no one worried about her absence, except her husband. In fact, for the first time in her life, people felt that Molly had done the sensible thing by keeping out of her husband's way. Doubtless when he returned to his ship, she would return to her home and collect her personal bits and pieces, because she had apparently left home in such a hurry, she had taken nothing with her but the clothes she was wearing.

On Wednesday morning, Gavin arrived at Tarris shortly before ten o'clock, and suggested that since it was such a glorious day, and since he had planned to go to Abbess Inch, the small island which lies near the centre of Loch Tarris, and which is a part of the Conynghame estate, to see Joe Tweedy, its only inhabitant, an elderly lobster fisherman, we might as well make a day of it and have a picnic on the island, whose sandy, crescent shaped cove, was ideal for bathing.

I was delighted at the prospect of a long, leisurely day in Gavin's company, and I went happily up to my bedroom to pack a beach bag with swim suits and the miscellany of things necessary for a day's outing, while Mrs Oliver volunteered to make up a food hamper for us.

"Don't pack too much food, Mrs Oliver," I heard Gavin say as I was running upstairs. "Mr Armstrong and Miss Burgess are coming with us, and Miss Burgess is bringing a variety of cold meats and the like, while Mr Armstrong has gone to buy cans of beer and fruit juice."

At his words a little of my bliss evaporated. I might have guessed that Gavin would not have been allowed to plan a day's *tête à tête* with me when Lois was in the neighbourhood. Or it might even have been Phyllis who had suggested the picnic, as something to give me some diversion on my holiday, and this was no doubt why Rory was making up the foursome.

I changed from the cotton dress I was wearing into a pair of pale blue denim jeans with a matching shirt, slipped on a pair of rope soled sandals, picked up my beach bag and hurried downstairs and along to the morning-room, where I could hear Gavin's voice above the sound of the vacuum cleaner which the daily help was using to clean the stair carpet, as he talked to Rory and Lois who had arrived while I was changing.

"I hope you have a lovely day," Phyllis said as she came to the door to see us off. She stood watching us, an envious look in her eyes, as we walked through the garden to the path which led steeply down to the cove on the western side of the promontory, where Grandfather had built a boathouse for the motor launch which in summer was as much used by the family as his Rover.

The cove is a small, natural, deep water harbour, well sheltered from the prevailing winds by the towering cliffs on three sides, and the scattering of half submerged rocks about fifty feet beyond the opening of the cove form an effective breakwater beyond which runs the strong current which carries rubbish and driftwood from the harbour of Tarrisdale a mile further up the coast, out to the Atlantic.

Lois was unexpectedly agile on her feet, and although a thick rope had been firmly anchored into the cliff face the length of the path to act as a handrail, she disdained its use apart from at one section where erosion had crumbled away the breadth of the path to a mere eighteen inches for a two yard stretch, and led the way at a running pace down to the boathouse, followed at a much more discreet pace by myself, with Gavin and Rory, carrying the picnic hampers, bringing up the rear.

Lois was careful to select a seat in the boat where she would get least spray and, after the men had stowed the hampers into a locker, she imperiously indicated to Gavin that he should come and sit beside her.

For a moment I thought he was going to refuse her request. It can be a tricky manoeuvre to steer the boat safely between the skerries and hidden reefs. You have to know not only the exact position of each hidden hazard, but also the currents and undertow as you emerge into the open loch. One false reckoning could mean disaster.

Gavin and I had both mucked about with boats since childhood, and knew every inch of the coastline within many miles either side of Tarrisdale, but after all, it had been five years since I had held a tiller and set out beyond the breakwater, and I would have understood if he had refused to delegate the task to me on this occasion.

However, after only a moment's hesitation, he nodded to me to take over, and I was thrilled to find that I had forgotten none of my "know how" as I steered the launch out through the narrow channel to the deeper waters of the loch.

Rory stripped off his blue cotton shirt and stretched himself along the wooden bench seat beside me, to enjoy the sunshine, and in their own corner Gavin and Lois conversed in low, intimate whispers.

I was curious to know what they were talking about so secretively, but soon the joy of being on the loch, feeling the launch bob up and down on the rippling waters, hearing the happy slap of the waves against the wooden hull, feeling the stinging salt of the spray on my cheeks and the warmth of the sun on my bare hands and arms, made me forget everything but the sheer delight of being alive, and skimming over Loch Tarris on this beautiful summer's day.

Looking back through the rainbow spray threshed up by the propeller along the greeny white wake which marked our passage, I could see the high cliffs of the promontory, and Tarris House, recede into the distance, and Tarrisdale, huddled round its little harbour looked even prettier than the postcards sold in the village shops. Even the great high mountains of the Tarris range seemed less austere and forbidding as they shimmered in the misty heat.

Ahead of us, still a quarter of an hour's trip away, the green eminence of Abbess Inch, with its ruined castle and woods of birches and larch, and the high, silvery stoned rock on the right of the castle which is the haunt of gannets and other sea birds, began to assume a more precise shape.

I could even make out the dark hollow which marked the entrance to the Giant's Cave, halfway up the cliff face, to which I had once climbed in search of sea gulls' eggs, and instead found Gavin and his current girl friend in each other's arms!

I smiled to myself as I remembered how furious they had both been. Gavin had accused me of always spying on him, and had described me to the girl, whose name I could not even remember now, as an accursed pest! I wondered if he remembered this particular incident, and still smiling, I turned to look at him, but Lois was still commanding his attention, and he was completely unaware of my look, and I sadly averted my gaze.

As we approached nearer to the island, I had to take great care to avoid the coloured plastic marker buoys which indicated where Joe had placed his lobster pots, and then I set the launch in line with the needle of rock, and reduced the engine speed to negotiate the entrance to the island bay, and bring the craft alongside the long stone jetty which juts some ten yards out into the loch.

At the change in the engine note, Rory lazily opened his eyes and sat up.

"Have we arrived already?" he looked around him. Then he stretched, tied his shirt by the sleeves round his neck, and came to stand beside me, with the boathook at the ready, as I manoeuvred the launch alongside the stone wall.

As Rory held the boat against the jetty with the hook, Gavin jumped ashore with the mooring rope and tied it fast to a wooden stanchion.

Lois was next to step on to the landing stage, and when she had done so, she turned to Rory to ask him to hand her her capacious beach bag which had been stored with the picnic hampers in the locker.

He did so, and she went strolling off down the jetty, while Rory retrieved the picnic boxes and handed them over to Gavin, who laid them on the stone cobbles and bent forward to give me a helping hand as I stepped up from the launch to the stone pier.

Lois led the way across the foreshore to the path which leads to the ruins of the old castle, which is the usual picnic spot, since it provides privacy for changing into beach clothes behind its thick walls, and also makes a wonderful suntrap for lazing in, sheltered from any breeze, and the great flat stones which have toppled from its battlements make the most convenient of tables and chairs for picnickers!

We decided to bathe first, have an early lunch, and then Gavin could go and visit Joe the lobster fisherman, whose house was on the far side of the island, while Rory, Lois and I sunbathed on the greensward of the castle forecourt.

Lois was not much of a swimmer, and preferred paddling about in the shallows to diving off the rocks at the entrance of the bay, and she seemed none too pleased when the three of us left her to her own devices while we went to have a race from one tip of the bay's crescent to the other.

When we eventually returned to the shore to towel ourselves dry, she was lying sunbathing on the sands, and her body, well oiled to protect her skin from the sun's rays, glistened like smooth, gold velvet, and under her chiffon net head scarf, I felt sure there was not a hair of her head out of place.

My skin was beginning to burn from over exposure to salt sea and sun, and I delved into my bag for a tube of suntan cream and somewhat belatedly started to apply it to my arms and neck and shoulders, but I could not quite reach the whole way round my back. Gavin watched my contortions for a few seconds, and then laughingly took the tube from me, saying:

"This was always my favourite job at picnics, remember, Joanna?"

Still smiling, he lavishly applied the cream all over my back and shoulders, and massaged it in, while Lois looked on, with narrowed eyes, and remarked sneeringly:

"It's rather late for that, Joanna. Your back is quite red already. I do hope it won't blister," she shivered delicately. "Blistering looks so unsightly!"

"Joanna won't blister!" said Gavin, firmly rubbing the grease into my shoulder blades. "She never was the fragile lily type," he added ungallantly, and giving me an equally ungallant smack on the buttocks went on: "There you are, child. That is my good deed for the day done!"

"And this is mine!" I retorted sweetly, tripping him up as he started to walk back to where Lois was lying, with the sneer on her face changing to a look of annoyance at Gavin's familiar slap. "Someone has to keep you in your place!"

"You little devil!" He staggered forward and fell on one knee in the sand, at the same time grabbing me by the ankle and pulling me down on the sand beside him, so that the brown-gold grit stuck to my damp swimsuit and oil-covered limbs in a most unpleasing way. "That will teach you!" he grinned.

"Oh!" I gasped, my mouth half full of sand, and staggered spluttering to my feet.

Still grinning, Gavin tripped me up once more.

It was the sort of silly, childish game we had often indulged in in those long ago summers of combined family picnics on the island, but Lois, who had not shared those days, obviously did not approve of our juvenile form of fun.

As I went floundering down on the sand for a third time, she spoke crossly.

"For goodness sake, stop playing the fool, you two! You are spraying sand all over me."

She rose to her feet and brushed furiously at the few specks of golden grit which had landed on her costume.

At her words, Gavin grimaced, but stopped teasing me, and Rory, sensing that I still planned to get my own back, caught hold of my hand as I moved towards Gavin, and firmly pulled me down to the water's edge.

"Come on, Joanna," he urged me forward with a smile. "Another quick swim will soon remove all evidence of the battle!"

Hand in hand we ran through the rippling shallows to the deeper waters of the loch, and as we ran thus, the curious thought crossed my mind that I seemed to be more emotionally conscious of Rory Armstrong's firm clasp on my fingers than I had been of Gavin's casually caressing touch as he oiled my back.

Even when Rory let go of my fingers to plunge ahead of me into the waves, I still seemed to feel the warm pressure of his hand on mine. It was an odd, but not unpleasant sensation, for which I could find no satisfactory explanation.

Chapter Fifteen

It took me some time to get rid of the sand which seemed glued to my body with the sun oil, and by the time Rory and I eventually returned from our extra swim, Lois was looking peevish.

"I am starving," she said reprovingly. "I think we should eat now."

She went strolling off towards the path which led to the ruins where we had left the picnic hampers, leaving Gavin to carry her bag. He caught my amused look as I watched him walking along with the vividly floral plastic container swinging from his hand, and grimaced back at me, with a none too pleased expression on his face.

When we reached the castle, we changed from our damp swimsuits, and while Lois and I placed a cloth over one of the flat stones which we had chosen for a table, and set out the paper plates and cups, and packets of food, the men lit a small fire with nearby brushwood.

The pleasant smell of cooking and wood smoke lent an edge to my appetite, which had already been whetted by the fresh air and exercise, and as well as eating the burnt sausages which Rory had skewered on the end of long twigs, and the over-roasted potatoes which were Gavin's offering, I enjoyed several of Mrs Oliver's famous sandwiches, which are made by slicing a long French loaf and stuffing it generously with honey baked ham, lettuce, tomatoes and chopped chives.

Lois, who was daintily nibbling at a cold chicken leg with her small, very white teeth, refused my offer of one of the sandwiches, and Gavin, who had been eyeing me as I tucked into the food, shook his head and said:

"I see you haven't lost your prodigious appetite, Joanna. I remember being fascinated by the amount of food you could put away, without adding an inch to your waist!"

"Wait until you are forty, Joanna!" teased Rory. "That is when it will show. You will make cook look like a sylph in comparison when you develop your middle aged spread!"

I laughed, and Lois, frowning because for the moment she was not the centre of attraction, tossed her half eaten chicken leg into a nearby clump of thistles, where it promptly attracted the attention of a score of bluebottles.

"Come along, Gavin!" She stood up. "Isn't it time you went to visit this man you came here specially to see? Rory and Joanna can tidy up and pack away the left-overs, and meet us at the boat in about an hour. I want to be home before five o'clock."

"That is when we were planning to be back," said Gavin. "My business with Joe won't take very long."

"I shouldn't mind having a crack with Joe myself," I said, standing up and brushing the crumbs from my shirt front.

I disliked Lois's dictatorial manner, as if she was the lady and we were the lackeys, and I saw no reason why she should have everything her own way.

"Joe would think it very rude of me if he knew I had come to Abbess Inch and hadn't bothered to visit him," I went on. "After all, it was he who taught me all that I know about sailing on Loch Tarris, and for that I shall always owe him a debt of gratitude."

"We shall all tidy up, carry the hampers back to the launch and go to Joe's together." Gavin for once did not give in to Lois. "In any case, it is easier to reach Joe's croft by walking round by the shore from the jetty than trailing across the island."

"That is a good idea!" I said with enthusiasm, turning to Rory. "Do you know that the shore here is quite a treasure trove? Apart from the things which get washed in by the tides, if you look hard enough, there is a chance of finding different types of chalcedony. Joe spends a lot of his spare time combing the beach, and he makes some very attractive jewellery from the stones which he picks up here, and polishes."

"Gavin, do you remember that lovely pendant that mother always wears? Joe made that from a piece of smoky quartz which I myself found near the cove where his croft is."

"Personally I think most of the jewellery made from the local stones is rather ugly," sneered Lois. "I simply cannot understand why so many people rave about it."

She watched for our reaction as we tidied away the remains of the picnic, and continued:

"I expect people just buy it because it is a different kind of holiday souvenir, and the recipients stow it at the back of a drawer out of sight!"

"That is nonsense!" I challenged her. "Joe makes some very attractive items, and everyone who has seen mother's pendant admires it."

Lois gave a disparaging shrug. "*Chacun a son goût*," she murmured, and strolled over to where she had put down her handbag, took out her compact, and renewed her make-up while we finished packing the hampers. Then Rory and Gavin carried them down to the launch, leaving Lois and I to follow them.

"It is a pity that Sally Henderson could not come today," observed Lois, watching for my reaction. "She and Rory are more than just good friends, wouldn't you say?"

"She seems equally friendly with Gavin," I remarked blandly. "In fact," I went on provocatively, "I would have thought that you were more Rory's type. Gavin used to prefer blondes!"

Her eyes narrowed to slits, but before she could reply the men waved to us to join them, and we set off together along the shore, although we did not keep together for long.

As if to show by her actions what she had not had time to say in words, Lois sidled up to Gavin, and possessively took his arm, so that he could help her over the rough stones.

I followed behind them, but soon became more absorbed in looking for pretty pebbles than in watching Lois's helpless little woman act.

Gavin and Lois arrived well ahead of us at the little croft with the thickly thatched roof which huddled against the hillside just above the high water mark.

A fat brown hen was picking about among the stones in front of the cottage, and a sleek marmalade cat had elected to take its afternoon siesta in the straggling bed of marigolds which brightened the garden patch on the lee side of the house.

As we drew near, it opened one wary eye, but when it realized that we had no intention of disturbing it, it let out one blissful burst of purring and resumed its nap.

We could see Joe in his boat about fifty yards out in the loch, pulling in his nets. He waved to us, and recognizing Gavin shouted:

"I'll no' be a moment, Mister Conynghame," and went on with his task.

It was a peaceful scene—the little cottage snuggled against the green, bracken covered hillside, the hen poking contentedly about its business, the cat asleep on its bed of gold, a butterfly sunning its brown wings on a creamy wild rose bloom, the old fisherman in his blue cap and jersey standing in his boat, slowly, almost lazily hauling in his catch.

There was a stillness about the setting that was soothing to the mind. Only the soft lapping of the loch waters on the shore and the soporific droning of the bees among the marigolds disturbed the quiet of the place, and we stood immobile, as if trapped for a moment in a hiatus of time.

The peace was shattered with alarming suddenness.

Joe gave a startled shout, muttered words which we could not distinguish, and began to pull more urgently on his net, but his haul must have been too big for him to tackle on his own, because he shouted to us again, and gesticulated, as if in need of assistance, then started the boat's motor, and with one hand still holding on to the net, very, very slowly, he brought his vessel to the shore.

Rory and I had been standing much farther back from the loch than the other two but there was something so urgent in Joe's actions that we automatically hurried forward to meet him at the water's edge.

The boat reached the shore, and Lois and Gavin stepped forward to pull it aground.

Then Lois let out a shocked cry, and stumbled forward, and would have collapsed into the water if Gavin had not made a grab at her.

She clung to him, whimpering, and even Gavin's face turned a grey/green shade as he looked down at the net, and Rory, who had had time to glimpse what I had not yet seen, exclaimed in horror, and pulled me back roughly, and told me to look the other way, but neither his action nor his warning was quick enough to prevent me seeing what Joe's haul was.

It was not an unusually heavy catch which was caught up in his net, nor was it, as for a second I had thought it might be, a discarded bundle of clothes from the tinker colony at the head of the loch.

It was the body of a woman.

Chapter Sixteen

Rory took charge of the situation. The first thing he did was to order me brusquely to look after Lois, while he and Joe turned their attention to the fisherman's tragic catch, and carefully tried to disentangle it from the mesh of the fishing net.

Gavin seemed momentarily paralysed, and for a moment I thought I was going to have two casualties on my hands. While I helped a stumbling Lois across the rocky shore to the stretch of greensward, where I made her sit down, Gavin continued to stare glassy-eyed at the two men who had to wade thigh deep into the water to perform their grim task.

A burst of inane laughter broke from Lois's quivering mouth, and I leaned down and slapped her sharply across the face.

The laughter stopped instantly. She instinctively put a hand up to touch her cheek, which must have been stinging from the impact of my blow. The blankness disappeared from her dark eyes, and was replaced by a look of such venom that I recoiled from her.

I could understand her reaction to my blow. It must have been mortifying for someone who regarded herself as poised and sophisticated and able to cope with any situation, to have broken down as she had done, and to have to be comforted by another woman, particularly a woman whom she had subtly made aware that she did not like.

"I'm sorry, Lois," I said gruffly. "It was for your own good."

She continued to regard me balefully, and I drew a deep breath and went on quickly:

"Do you think you can stand up now? I think we should go back to the launch. There is still some coffee in one of the flasks. A hot drink will do us both good."

Slowly she rose to her feet, and with an effort which was visible, she pulled herself together.

"I am sorry," she said in a low tone as Gavin, with the other two men, came towards us. "I have never seen a dead—a dead body before," she stuttered.

Then she gave a little moan and ran forward into Gavin's arms and pressed her face against his shoulder. A shudder convulsed her whole body as she whimpered, "Gavin, hold me tight! I feel so awful!"

Gavin held her close in his arms, and whispered soothingly to her, although he himself was still looking shaken and shocked by the tragedy.

I noticed that both Rory and Joe had a whitish tinge to their sunburnt features, and I was not feeling too good myself. Like Lois, at that moment I could have done with a little comforting, but I didn't have a shoulder to cry on.

"Joanna," Rory's voice was low, but commanding. "Do you think you could take the boat back to Tarrisdale, and tell Sergeant Dougal about this? Take Lois home at the same time."

He glanced across at the other couple. "Poor lass, she is not nearly so hard boiled as she makes out to be," he added sympathetically.

What about poor me? I thought angrily, as returning nausea made me feel cold and clammy and for a moment I thought I was going to pass out. I clenched my teeth tightly together and willed the faintness away.

I was not any more used to dead bodies than Lois was, and I felt every bit as upset as she did, but I was too proud to show my weakness. However, I was glad that Rory had asked me to do something definite, because action would keep my mind off what I had seen, and with a final gulping away of the incipient bout of sickness, I replied, albeit somewhat shakily.

"Certainly I shall take Lois home. But aren't you coming too?"

He shook his head.

"I think I had better wait here with Joe until the police arrive."

"What about Gavin?" I prompted.

"I was going to ask him to stay on," Rory glanced across at the other two, "but I think he had better go with you to keep an eye on Lois in case she has another fit of hysteria. There is a fairly strong current at the mouth of Tarrisdale harbour, as I learned to my cost the first time I went sailing there, and you will need all your wits about you to negotiate the bar, without having to deal with a hysterical woman at the same time."

He smiled at me gravely.

"Thank goodness you managed to keep a level head, Joanna," he said approvingly. "But then," he looked at me in a way which made me feel quite shaky again, but for an entirely different reason, "I rather thought you would!"

Some of the grimness smoothed from his face.

"No wonder your grandfather has always spoken so well of you."

He continued to look at me in such a way that I flushed and dropped my eyes, and I could have hugged Joe for coming over to us and breaking the peculiar tension of the moment.

"You had best get on your way as soon as you can, Miss Fraser," he advised, pointing to the west, where the blue of the sky was beginning to darken over with lowering, copper-fringed clouds. "There is a storm brewing, and the police will want to have their work here over and done with before it breaks."

I hurried back to the launch, and Gavin followed on my heels, helping a still white faced Lois over the more rugged parts of the shore.

When we reached the boat, I jumped in, followed by Lois, while Gavin undid the rope from the stanchion, and waited until I had started the engine, before joining us.

Lois huddled down in a corner behind the spray screen, where she was sheltered from the freshening wind, and Gavin sat down beside her, and put a comforting arm round her shoulders. She snuggled against him, and clung to his hand for the whole of the trip.

When we neared the quayside at Tarrisdale, Gavin gently released himself from her clasp, and stood up to get the boat hook to guide the launch alongside. Then he jumped on to the cobbles of the pier and tied the mooring rope to one of the iron rings cemented into the quayside for this purpose.

Lois held out her hands for him to stretch down and help her up beside him, and she stood leaning against him, shaking slightly, as if she was still not quite herself.

I clambered out of the launch and joined them.

"Joanna," Gavin appealed to me. "Would you mind taking Lois home, and seeing she is all right? I shall go along to the police station and tell them what has happened."

Lois looked none too pleased at this arrangement, but made no demur.

"How about the launch?" I asked. "Will you take it back to the Tarris boathouse, or shall I?"

"I may have to go back to Abbess Inch with the police," said Gavin slowly. "It should be all right here."

I looked westwards towards the massing thunder clouds.

"I shall see if I have time to take it back to

the boathouse myself, before the storm breaks, after seeing to Lois."

"And I had better hurry along to the station," Gavin turned to Lois. "I shall look in and see how you are feeling later this evening." He strode off.

I covered the half mile to the Burgess's house at about half my usual speed. Lois walked like an automaton, slowly and rigidly, her eyes fixed blankly on the road ahead. When we reached her home, a rambling old house which stood on its own in an unkempt garden at the edge of Lower Tarris Wood, she spoke for the first time.

"Father has gone to Fort William for the day. I don't expect he will be home until late." She bit her lip. "I don't feel like going into the house on my own, silly, isn't it?" She hesitated. "Would you mind coming in with me, please?"

It must have taken quite an effort for Lois to ask a favour of me, and I did not like to say that I wanted to get back to the launch as quickly as possible, to take it round to the boathouse cove before it got too stormy to cross the bar, so I followed her into the gloomy hall and the even gloomier sitting-room, which, with its worn and faded turkey red carpet and sagging settee looked as if its better days had been a long, long time ago.

Lois indicated the more comfortable looking of the fireside chairs.

"Sit down for a few minutes, Joanna. I shall go and make a coffee."

"No! You sit down, and I shall make the coffee, if you tell me where to find things," I offered.

Lois shook her head.

"No. I shall feel better if I have something to do!"

She hurried out of the room, closing the door behind her.

Chapter Seventeen

I sat down and looked about me with curiosity. This was not at all the kind of background that I associated with Lois.

The room was shabby, and had been decorated with little taste. It was in need of repapering and painting, but there were one or two beautiful pieces of furniture which had been polished with care, to bring out the pattern of the graining, and on a half moon table, with a claw-footed pedestal, an opaline bowl, filled with purple and pink sweet peas, showed that Lois was trying to bring some charm into a room which had been long neglected.

On the side table beside my chair there was a number of society magazines and a cuttings book.

Idly I picked up the book. It was full of photographs of Lois at various stages of her career, from leading lady at her school's amateur dramatic production, to snaps taken during debutante balls; from cuttings of her standing outside stately homes which she had helped to redecorate, talking to the stately owners, to a full page spread from the local paper of her attending a garden party at Holyrood House with her father, and to others showing her on the fringe of the crowd when Phyllis and grandfather were welcoming ashore a party from the Royal yacht when it had paid a visit to Tarrisdale earlier in the summer.

I replaced the scrap book and picked up one of the magazines, but found little to interest me in the groups of unknowns attending this and that social function, and I was about to lay it down again when Lois came into the room carrying a tray set with two cups of steaming coffee.

"I have put a spot of brandy in them both," she announced. "For all your outward calm, you are probably feeling every bit as shaken as I do," she went on. "And I am sure if you had had as close a look at the body as I had, you would have been much more upset."

"I am sure I should," I replied, gratefully taking the cup she proffered. "On first sight, all I saw as what seemed to be a bundle of old clothes, tied with a blue scarf. I had only the briefest glimpse of a face before Rory pulled me back."

"Did you recognize her?"

"Why, no!"

"It was Molly Mackay," said Lois flatly.

"Molly!" I gasped. "Oh, no!" My eyes dilated with horror. "Are you sure? I thought it might be one of the old tinker women from the camp."

"It was Molly," repeated Lois harshly. "That is why Gavin was so terribly upset. I expect that you knew she was one of his first girl friends?"

"That is right! I had almost forgotten about it," I replied slowly. "Poor Molly! To think I was once wildly jealous of her!"

"So I believe!" The trace of malice in Lois's voice showed that she was recovering rapidly. "Gavin told me that you used to trail him around all over the place when you were young. He found your devotion most embarrassing!"

"Did he?" I shrugged nonchalantly. "Funny, I had forgotten about that! Still apparently he must have been impressed by my attachment to talk about it!"

I felt that I had turned the tables very neatly, because Lois hastily reverted to the subject of Molly's death.

"She must have been in an awful state to drown herself," she eyed me over the rim of her cup.

"To drown herself!" I repeated her last words incredulously. "What makes you think she drowned herself? Her death was an accident, surely!"

"I wonder!" Lois shook her head doubtfully. "She was terrified of her husband at the best of times," she laid the coffee cup on the tray. "You know the way he treated her!"

"Yes. But—"

"I don't think there are any buts," Lois interrupted. "She knew that after what happened, Mackay was bound to hear of her affair with the lorry driver, and she was probably frightened out of her wits as to how he would treat her when he found out."

"She didn't need to drown herself!" I protested. "She could have run away somewhere." My voice trailed off. Where could someone like Molly, with no friends outside of Tarrisdale and no money of her own run to?

I remembered what Rory had said. That Molly Mackay was one of those people who are born victims. How right he had been.

My blood ran cold at the thought of what this girl, so very little older than myself, had been driven to, and I gulped at the hot, strong coffee to warm me up.

Suddenly I wanted to get away from Lois. I did not want to sit on in this gloomy room and discuss the tragedy. I wanted to get outside, into the fresh air, and do something to take my mind off what had happened.

"Lois," I set the cup on the tray. "If you think you will be all right on your own now, would you excuse me? I want to get back to the harbour and return the launch to Tarris boathouse before the storm comes any nearer."

Lois stood up and lifted my beach bag from the floor beside my chair.

"How long will that take you?" she asked as I rose to my feet.

"At least thirty minutes. To get safely round the promontory when the wind is blowing from the west, I have to steer fairly far out into the loch to avoid the skerries."

"I don't envy you," she said, handing me my beach bag, which burst open as I took it, sending the contents spilling over the floor.

"I am sorry!" exclaimed Lois, bending down to retrieve the fallen articles and shove them back in the bag. "I still feel very shaky. Once you leave, I am going to my room to swallow a couple of sleeping pills and lie down. I think that is the best thing for me to do, don't you?" She ushered me out.

I hurried back to the harbour, which was already beginning to fill up with smaller pleasure craft and a few fishing boats. From the west, ominous grumbles of thunder could be heard muttering over the mountain tops, and overhead great gulls wheeled and screamed as if they too were giving warning of the approaching storm.

The water in the harbour had that peculiar, viscous look it gets in the moments before summer storms, and there was an electric tension in the air which urged me to cast off the mooring rope and get on my way as quickly as possible.

I was rounding the promontory when the first large drops of rain spattered across the water towards me and streamed across my back with icy coldness, quickly soaking through the thin fabric of my blouse.

Under the hull of the launch, the loch seethed with the promise of the tempestuous waves to come, and the racing tide tried to draw me into the minor maelstrom between the skerries on my right, but the powerful engine of the craft kept me on course.

Although the sky to the east was still a lovely, clear turquoise, the thunder clouds were already lowering over Abbess Inch, and I wondered if the police had managed to get to the island, and complete whatever business they had to do there.

I hoped so, because if they had not, when the storm struck, they would be marooned on the island, and have to spend the night there, crowded into Joe's little croft, which is the only habitable dwelling there.

I steered my way from the turbulent waters of the loch through the narrow passage which led to the cove, and shutting off the engine, glided smoothly into the boathouse, where I made everything storm fast.

Then I picked up my beach bag and emerged from the shelter of the sturdy boathouse into a blustering downpour.

I bent my head before the gale and began the steep scramble up the narrow, rock-strewn path to the house. If it had not been for the stout rope stapled into the rock face to serve as a hand rail, I would have made very little progress, but with its help I was able to haul myself up the track, down which the water was now streaming, making each step I took slippery and treacherous.

Every now and then a miniature landslide of earth and stones, loosened from the path by the torrential rain, came tumbling down the path almost knocking me off my feet, but I clung to the rope with grim determination and struggled on.

My palms were scorched with the harshness of the cord, and my vision was blinded by the deluge, so that I could only see about a step ahead of me at a time.

At last I reached the most difficult part of the ascent, and before tackling it, I decided to stop and draw breath.

Far below me I could hear the waves crash against the base of the cliff, and I shuddered as I thought what one faulty step, one accidental slip, could mean.

Perhaps it was my reluctance to move forward, or perhaps it was my automatic adoption of the precept my grandfather had drummed into me when we had gone climbing together in the mountains, that one should never take safety for granted—whatever the reason, before I moved forward past the next rung which secured the rope to the cliff face, I gave a tug on the rope to test its strength at this point.

It didn't seem as taut as it should be. I frowned, and instinctively holding more securely to the sturdy rung beside which I stood, I gave the rope a stronger tug to test it once more.

As I did so, the rope suddenly gave way altogether, and in front of my appalled eyes, went snaking down over the edge of the precipice.

Cold as I was in my sodden clothes, I became colder still as I realized that if I had committed my full weight to this section of rope without first testing it, as I very well might not have done, I would have been yanked off my feet as it came loose from its rung, and gone hurtling down into the crashing waves far below.

Chapter Eighteen

I don't know how long I stood there, my face pressed against the smooth, streaming wet surface of the cliff face, before the paralysis of shock stole from my limbs.

With the return of sensation, my teeth started to chatter uncontrollably, and tears of panic mingled with the rain which flowed down my cheeks.

I knew I could not remain where I was indefinitely, and so inch by inch, testing and double testing the ground under each step I took, and pressing close to the cliff wall, I retraced my way down the track as far as its juncture with the original path to the cove, which led from behind the orchard at Tarris House, by a long, meandering trail through upper Tarris Wood, along the far side of the promontory and down an easier, but more circuitous path between mighty boulders and through a narrow, weather eroded archway in the rock wall, to join the present path, which had first been put into use by my grandfather when he had built the boathouse in the cove, and which in spite of its steepness, was more convenient, and had been made, as he thought, safe, by affixing the rope hand rail.

Anyone who had not lived at Tarris before the boathouse had been built would not have known of the original path, and even I had forgotten about it until reminded by necessity. I had certainly forgotten what a long and rambling and roundabout way it was, and it was at least half an hour after I set out on it that I trudged up the front steps of Tarris House, looking as woebegone as a half drowned cat.

Rory met me at the front door.

He was in a blazing temper.

"Where the devil have you been all this time?" he demanded angrily. "You have had us all extremely worried."

Phyllis, who had been standing behind him, also looked at me with cold reproach.

"It was extremely thoughtless of you, Joanna, not to come home before this. Your grandfather has been asking for you, and knowing Rory is home from the picnic, he cannot understand why you have not been to see him to tell him about your outing."

"We dared not tell him that you had not been seen since you left Tarrisdale harbour to return to the cove in the launch," Rory interrupted her. "Don't you realize how your lack of consideration could have affected him?"

I stood inside the threshold of the hall, the water from my hair trickling uncomfortably down the back of my neck, and the water from my soaking clothes and squelching espadrilles forming spreading pools around my feet and staining the beautiful polish of the parquet floor, and I gaped at them in dismay for their uncalled-for diatribes.

"I am sorry if I have upset you," I began, "but I could not help being so late."

"You couldn't help being late!" reiterated Rory. "You mean you just didn't think, and went gallivanting off on some silly ploy of your own, without telling anyone where you were off to! You must have realized that we would worry about you when we thought you out on the loch with a storm raging."

"I was safely in the cove before the wind blew up to any great force," I glared back at him. "Anyway, I would have been back an hour ago, if whoever is responsible for checking on the security of the rope rail on the path had been doing his job properly. Because it had given way, I had to come back to Tarris by the old path, and since you probably don't know it, let me tell you it is an extremely long and roundabout one!"

I sneezed violently.

"Now, if you have both finished with your cross-examinations," I looked from one to the other, "may I go to my room and change into some dry clothes, before I freeze to death?"

Head in air I flounced off, ignoring the appeal in Phyllis's voice as she called after me, "Joanna, please! Wait a minute!" and continuing to hasten up the stairs to my room.

I stripped off my wet clothes, dropped them in the laundry basket in the bathroom, and warmed the chill from my bones in a steaming hot bath.

I was annoyed with Phyllis for thinking that I would have deliberately done something to upset grandfather, and angrier still with Rory for the dressing down he had given me before he had even given me time to explain my absence. Who did he think he was, to talk to me like that?

I dressed quickly and returned downstairs, to find Rory, Gavin and Phyllis standing in the hall beside the newly lit log fire, with sherry glasses in their hands.

"Is it in order for me to go and see my grandfather now?" I asked her coldly.

I was being childishly rude in my attitude, but I had resented the way I had been taken to task the moment I had arrived back from that wearisome trek from the cove, and I have never been very good at hiding my feelings.

Phyllis looked uncomfortable.

"Of course, Joanna," she said in a placatory tone. "You know you can go in to see Hugh any time you wish. Actually I told him that you had returned, and had gone to change from your sailing clothes before you went in to see him."

"Joanna, you should not have taken the launch from the harbour by yourself, when you saw the storm that was brewing up!" It was now Gavin's turn to reprove me. "I intended to take it back to the cove myself the moment I arrived back from Abbess Inch with Rory. Apparently we missed you by only a matter of minutes."

I smiled at him, ignoring the other two.

"Gavin!" I reproached him. "You should have

known not to worry about me! I have taken the launch in and out of the cove as often as you have! I could do it blindfold!"

"It is five years since you sailed here, Joanna. After all that time, you could have misjudged the channel. When Rory telephoned me and said you had not shown up at Tarris, I was every bit as worried as he and Phyllis were."

"You need never worry about me!" I assured them. "I have always been able to look after myself."

"I hope you are right about that," Rory was still unsmiling.

"Of course I am!" I retorted lightly. "Now, if you will all excuse me, I shall go and have my chat with grandfather."

I turned and walked across to grandfather's room, conscious that for the moment I was the cynosure of three pairs of faintly disapproving eyes.

Grandfather beamed with pleasure when I entered his room.

"I thought you had gone off and deserted me again, Joanna!" he greeted me. "It has seemed such a long day without a visit from you. I am getting used to having you home again!"

I sat down on the edge of his bed.

"Don't tell me you have read all the books Rory and I bought you!" I chaffed him.

"I get tired of reading, especially when the sun streams through my window, as it did for the greater part of the day." He sighed. "How I was envying you your trip to Abbess Inch. I could not help remembering all the picnics we used to have there—you, your mother and your grandmother. The weather always seemed to be good in those long ago summer days. Not like now, when you can't depend on it from one hour to the next."

"So it is quite true that one only remembers the good days!" I teased him. "What about all the times we had to postpone our picnics even then, because of the sudden storms?"

"There were so many good times!" he mused. "But tell me. How did you enjoy yourself today?"

I managed to stifle an incipient sneeze before I replied.

"I got a good touch of the sun, while it lasted. A few more days like this, and I shall be as brown as I would have been if I had gone to Italy!"

"That is where you meant to spend your summer holiday, wasn't it?"

I nodded. "In Venice."

"Venice," he repeated the name. "That is where your grandmother and I spent our honeymoon. At the Danieli. She thought it wonderful and romantic, and so it was. We saw it at its best, in May, before the tourist season really got under way. Every morning, I remember, I used to buy her bunches of carnations from the flower seller in the Piazza, until the chambermaid complained she was running out of vases!"

He sighed. "It seems such a long, long time ago. A lifetime ago." His eyes had the far away look of happiness remembered, and I said nothing to break the spell.

A quiet knock on the door eventually disturbed his reverie. Phyllis came into the room carrying his supper tray.

"There is still time for you to have a sherry with Rory and Gavin before Mrs Oliver sounds the gong, Joanna," she smiled at me.

"I shall come back later to say goodnight, grandfather." I squeezed his hand affectionately.

"Tell Gavin I should like to see him for a moment before he leaves, will you my dear? I have been thinking of this idea of his for draining the marshes for his bulbs, and I think I have got a better way."

"Really, Hugh!" Phyllis chided him. "You know what the doctor said. You are not to worry about the management of the estate. It is in very good hands."

I left her fussing over him, and went out to join the two men who were standing chatting in front of the fire.

As I approached, the sneezing fit which I had managed to control while with grandfather, triumphed, and Rory looked at me keenly.

"I hope you haven't caught a cold after the soaking you had this afternoon," he said, and bypassing the decanter of sherry, he poured some brandy into a glass for me.

"Here, take this!" He handed it to me. "You don't want to spend the rest of your holiday in bed."

"I think it is more a touch of hay fever than

anything else," I replied. "I have always been allergic to fennel, and there was a lot of it in bloom at Abbess Inch."

Before I took the glass, Rory held it up to the light beside my hair, which was drying out and beginning to curl in loose ringlets at the nape of my neck.

"I was right! Your hair is almost brandy coloured!"

"And like brandy," Gavin teased me, "it improves with age! As a youngster, I would have likened it more to sea tangle and it was always as limp and wet!"

I had the feeling that Gavin's chaff was to try to keep my mind off the events of the afternoon, but I could not bottle up my curiosity any longer.

"Tell me, what did the police say about Molly? Lois thinks she committed suicide!"

"Nonsense!" Gavin's lips tightened, and he turned and stared into the fire. "It must have been an accident."

"They say she had been in the water for several days," said Rory.

"How horrible!" I shuddered. "And to think that all that time, everyone merely thought she had run away from her husband."

"Joanna! Stop talking about it, will you?" rapped Gavin sharply. "There will be enough tittle tattle about her in the village, without you adding your quota."

I stared at him in surprise. I had never known Gavin so touchy. He was bound to be affected to a certain degree by the girl's death, but his infatuation for Molly had been over and done with years ago. As Sally had hinted, Gavin must be more sensitive about things than I had imagined.

Now, although I was naturally curious to hear the police opinion about the affair, I said nothing more, but I could not help wondering if perhaps Lois had been right. Knowing that her husband was bound to hear about the theft of the lorry and so find out about her affair with Harry Brook, had she been less afraid of death than of the brutal beating she knew would ensue?

I cradled the brandy glass in my hands and stared bleakly into the amber liquid.

Poor Molly. The born victim.

Slowly I sipped my drink. I could think of nothing to say to shake off the mood of despondency which had come over Gavin, and even Rory looked at him with puzzled eyes, and seemed as relieved as I was when Mrs Oliver sounded the dinner gong and broke the uncomfortable spell.

There was only one reference made about the incident at dinner, and that was by Phyllis, who thanked me for not worrying her husband by mentioning what had happened to him.

"I meant to warn you to say nothing before you went in to see him," she said, "but—" she hesitated.

"But I was on my high horse! I know!" I smiled a shamefaced apology. "I was annoyed with the way you had taken me to task the minute I came in the door after my perfectly awful walk in the storm, and I did not take time to think that indignation was engendered by a genuine concern for my grandfather."

I looked at them both in turn. "I am sorry," I apologized once more.

"That is one thing about Joanna," commented Gavin. "She never sulks for long, and she is always willing to admit when she has been in the wrong."

"Life is too short to waste time on overmuch self pity!" I retorted lightly, but even as I carelessly spoke the words, the smile faded from my face as I remembered how very short life had been for another girl, not much older than myself.

It seemed impossible, somehow, to dismiss Molly from my mind, and although her name was never mentioned and we talked of other matters, I think the rest of the party shared my thoughts.

After dinner, Gavin went in to have a chat with grandfather. Phyllis excused herself and went upstairs to her studio, and Rory, after restlessly rustling through the evening paper, and stating that there did not seem to be a thing worth watching on television, asked if I would like to go for a walk in the garden with him, to get a breath of fresh air before bedtime.

The storm had blown itself out, and although there were still a few clouds in the sky, with their edges stained a livid red from the setting sun, it looked bright and pleasant out of doors.

Like Rory, I too felt restless. I could not understand why, for never before had I felt so completely unsettled at Tarris. I belonged here, yet somehow I felt as if I was an intruder. Even Rory seemed more at home in my old home than I did now, and I wondered if that was how he thought of Tarris—as his home.

I went upstairs for a stole to cover my bare arms against the cool of the evening. I hoped by the time I came down again, Gavin would have finished his talk with grandfather and joined us on our walk, but it was only Rory who awaited me at the foot of the stairs, and I felt somewhat self conscious as Mrs Oliver came out of the dining-room and watched us go out together, with a look of approval in her eyes.

We strolled through Phyllis's rose garden, avoiding the puddles left by the torrential rain of the late afternoon, wandered along the meandering path which led through the shrubbery, and inevitably, or so it seemed, we came out at the top of the promontory, close to the path which led to the boathouse.

We stood for a time, gazing out over the loch in admiration of the wonderful mixture of sunset colours mingled in its waters, and then, doubtless impelled by curiosity, Rory wandered off down the path to see how much damage had been done to it by the storm.

I stood waiting for him to return, and when he came back after a few minutes, he was frowning.

"I would never have thought that a mere deluge could have caused such havoc. Apart from the collapse of one of the rungs which secure the rope rail, several feet of pathway have crumbled completely away! Thank goodness you were not on it when it disintegrated!"

"You can say that again!" I shivered as I thought what my fate might have been.

"Your guardian angel seems to be working overtime at the moment." Rory's lips were unsmiling. "Three near accidents in under a week! No wonder you were so ungracious this evening when we berated you for being late!"

"You would almost think that someone at Tarris was wanting me out of the way!" I gave a shaky laugh.

Rory glanced at me sharply.

"Don't be silly!" he snapped. "Why should anyone here want that? Everyone is delighted to see you home again."

He took my arm and led me firmly from the cliff top.

"The trouble with you, Joanna, is that you have too much imagination," he spoke angrily. "You are probably one of those people who are more accident prone than others, so you will have to watch out in future!"

From his tone I did not know whether he was teasing me or actually warning me, and since the setting sun was behind us, I could not make out the expression on his face.

We arrived back at the house as Gavin was leaving.

"I am going to call on Lois on my way home

and see how she is feeling now," he said. "I called on my way up, but got no reply."

"You may still get no reply," I said. "She was going to take some sleeping pills and lie down, and her father was not due back from Fort William until late."

"Poor Lois is highly strung," said Gavin sympathetically. "It is a good thing she had the sense to go and lie down, but a pity there is no one at home to look after her just now." He gave my ringlets a friendly tug.

"Goodnight, Joanna. See you sometime."

To my surprise, Rory also wished me a rather curt goodnight, and went off to Tarrisdale with Gavin.

Chapter Nineteen

I did not sleep well that night. Visions of Molly Mackay floating from the fishing net, her hair tangled with scum and drifting weed half covering her death mask face, and the sodden chiffon of her blue scarf trailing like a streamer behind her, kept recurring each time I closed my eyes.

At one point I woke up, cold with excitement because in my dream something which I had noticed that morning had slipped into context, startling me awake with its implication, but the suddenness of my waking sent the thought back into limbo and try as I might, I could not recall it again.

Yet it was important. I was teasingly aware of

this. It had something to do with the cliff path and my accident with the lorry. A common factor to both. What had it been?

I tossed and turned in my vain endeavour to recall the incident, and although from sheer tiredness I would doze off momentarily, I would soon waken again, my mind too restless with its problem to let me sink to a more profound sleep.

Early dawn sparked the sky with flaming gold and early birdsong filled the air with melody.

I closed my eyes to the light and my ears to the sweet carolling, but I could not close my mind to the puzzle which kept nagging at me.

I wondered if a visit to the cliff path would trigger off the memory, and since sleep seemed no longer possible, I decided to put this idea to the test.

I slipped out of bed, dressed hastily, and with extreme caution, tip-toed from my room and out of the house.

I crossed the flagged courtyard, making for the path which led to the cove. The morning breeze ruffled through my hair and scattered the petals of the overfull rose blooms across the ground like confetti.

Behind me, I heard a faint tapping sound, as if someone was trying to attract my attention from the house.

I looked round with disquiet. Who else could be up at this unusual hour of the morning?

The curtains of grandfather's room downstairs were still drawn, as were the curtains of the rooms on the upper floor, bar one, and it was from the window of this room that the tapping came.

Rory was standing there, pulling on his blue pullover and signalling to me to wait for him.

I bit my lip with annoyance. What I wanted to look for, if I hadn't been imagining things, I wanted to look for by myself. I hesitated for a few seconds, and then started forward again, but before I reached the path which led to the cove, Rory, who must have moved with the speed of an athletic champion, had made up on me.

"What on earth are you doing up at this hour, Joanna?" he challenged me.

"I could not sleep."

"Neither could I," he said, falling into step beside me. "Is there something troubling you?"

"I kept thinking about Molly, and—"

"And?"

"Nothing really. My over-imaginative mind at work again, I should think." I smiled.

"Imagining what?" he scowled.

"I don't know! That is the annoying part! Do you ever feel that you have the answer to a mystery, without even knowing that there is a mystery?"

"I never put the cart before the horse!" he chaffed me. "Are you sure you were not dreaming? How about a swim before breakfast?" he suggested. "That should chase the cobwebs away!"

"That sounds a wonderful idea!" I felt suddenly lighthearted.

"I shall go and get my car then, and we can

drive to the little sandy bay at the far side of Tarrisdale."

"You know your way around here pretty well, don't you?"

"There is very little else to do in Tarrisdale, except walk or hill climb or swim or sail, is there?"

"You must enjoy walking and swimming and sailing to come here so often. Or is there some other attraction?" I asked him, remembering the way he had left me so abruptly last night to go down to the village.

"You are a curious young woman, aren't you?" he smiled. "What other attraction would there be?"

I wanted to say Sally Henderson, but at the same time, for some reason I could not explain to myself, I did not want him to confirm my suspicions, so instead, I said, with a shrug, "That is what I was asking you!"

He made no reply as I followed him into the back garden of the house, where our swimming costumes had been hung over a rope on the drying green, to dry out overnight.

We drove to the bay, which was empty, except for a few gulls which were scavenging along the high water mark.

The water seemed icy cold, and it took my breath away as I surface dived into the waves, but soon I was enjoying my swim, and the exhilaration of the exercise dispelled my tiredness and drove away my chimeras.

As I briskly towelled my arms and legs dry on

the beach, Rory, who had left the water a few minutes before I had, and who had already dried himself and changed from his swimming trunks to flannels and his cotton pullover, was sitting on a flattish slab of sandstone, watching the flight of a large gull as it soared and swooped high in the heavens, its body and wings forming a moving white cross against the deepening blue of the morning sky.

I went to the car to change, and when I returned to the beach, Rory was still staring, absorbed, at the bird's flight.

I walked to the water's edge in my bare feet and rinsed the sand from my swimming costume. Everything was so quiet and peaceful, I thought, smiling at the fancy, that we two could have been alone on a desert island.

I spread my costume on a nearby rock and went over to squat down on the sand beside Rory.

"Feeling better?" he glanced at me. "You look it," he went on. "Now no one would know that you had spent a restless night."

"The same applies to you," I countered. "But then, perhaps you are used to burning the candle at both ends. I heard you come in fairly late last night."

He stood up and stretched himself lazily before he replied.

"I am used to a topsy turvy world of time," he observed as he bent down to help me to my feet. "You get to be, in my job."

"So you are not a regular nine to five

worker?" I looked at him quizzically. "Somehow I did not think that you were. What do you work at, Rory?"

He seemed surprised at my question.

"Don't you know? I thought your grandfather might have mentioned it to you. He thinks I have a most interesting job. I am an airline pilot."

"Oh!" I looked at him with envious eyes. "You are lucky. You must see a great many different countries and peoples. Or do you get blasé about it all?"

"It is a job I set my heart on achieving when I was at College." He opened the boot and put in our towels and bathing gear. "I love flying. Next year, all going well, and if I have saved enough money to be able to afford it, I want to enter for the air race from London to Melbourne."

"You lucky man!" I breathed, getting into the car. "I have always wanted to learn to fly myself, but mother, naturally, was against it."

"When is your mother due home?"

"I am not very sure, but it will not be long now. She will probably get in touch right away when she knows where I am. I wouldn't even be surprised if she came straight here, bringing her new husband with her to meet her father."

"Is your mother like you at all?" asked Rory curiously as we drove past the harbour and up the steep hill which led to Tarris House.

"I would say that Gavin is more like her than I am, in appearance, and," I shook my head, "certainly in temperament. They are both Conynghames in their pride, their determination to get their own way, their tempers—whereas, as everyone is well aware, I take after my grandmother's side of the family."

"The Conynghame's are a stubborn breed, aren't they?" agreed Rory. "I remember your grandfather would not take "No" for an answer from mother when he asked her to marry him. Gavin has the same streak in him, I have noticed. When he wants a thing, he goes after it with dour determination!" He shook his head. "I should hate to stand in his way if he really set his heart on something!"

"Is that why you don't flirt with Lois?" I teased him.

"Lois isn't my type, as I told you once before," he glanced at me.

"I wouldn't have thought she was Gavin's type either, at least, not for a permanent affair. In fact, I would have thought he had had enough of being bossed around by his mother to want to have another domineering female for his life's partner. He deserves better than that!"

"Perhaps an infatuated blonde would be better?" he mocked me.

I ignored the mockery. "He always used to prefer blondes, like Molly—" I stopped short and stared ahead of me.

I had not wanted to think of Molly again. I had wanted to forget about her, but how can one forget the face that has haunted one's dreams?

There was silence between us for the rest of the journey, and even during breakfast we hardly spoke. It was as if mention of the drowned girl's name had cast a blight on our pleasant morning.

After breakfast I went to see grandfather. When I told him that Rory and I had been swimming together at the crack of dawn, he looked pleased.

"I am so glad you two are getting on well together." He stroked the purring tabby which had settled on the bed beside him. "Rory is a very fine young man. Wouldn't it be—" he broke off as Phyllis came into the room to tell me that I was wanted on the telephone.

"It is Lois," she informed me.

"Lois?" I frowned. "I wonder what she wants?"

Lois was all apologies for disturbing me, but she had just found my lipstick in her hall, where it must have rolled when my beach bag had burst open the previous evening.

"Shall I bring it to you now, or get Gavin to take it up later?" she asked.

"I hadn't even noticed it was missing, and I have another one the same shade, so there is no hurry to return it," I assured her. "How are you feeling this morning?"

"Almost my usual self, thank goodness," she replied. "I had a really good night's sleep, which seemed to do the trick, and I didn't waken up from the time you saw me until father came to my room with breakfast this morning!"

"That was good," I murmured politely, but she interrupted me to add:

"What do you think of the latest development in the Molly affair?"

"What development?"

"Haven't you heard?" she exclaimed. "Father had it direct from Sergeant Dougal, so it must be true.

"The result of the post mortem showed that Molly was dead before she was put into the loch. She was strangled with that ridiculous chiffon scarf she always affected!"

Chapter Twenty

We had said nothing to grandfather the previous evening about the finding of Molly Mackay's body in Joe's fishing net, but now it was impossible to keep the news of the murder from him for it made front page news in the local edition of the daily paper to which he subscribes.

He was most upset about the affair, because he had known the girl, but he was even more upset by the police activity which the murder triggered off.

When Lois had told me her news on the telephone that morning, I had jumped to the obvious conclusion that poor Molly had been killed by her husband in a fit of rage when he had found out about her affair with Harry Brook, but apparently this was not so.

According to the experts who had performed

the post mortem examination, Molly had been killed sometime after she had eaten her supper on Friday night, and before breakfast the following morning, and at this time her husband, Ken Mackay, had been on board a trawler on the North Sea, with an entire ship's crew to testify as to his presence there, and he was one of the few people concerned with Molly who had a perfect alibi.

With no other suspect, the police were now questioning every man who had been out and about in Tarrisdale about the times in question, and their list of men to be interviewed included, among a number of others, both Rory and Gavin.

Rory had soon satisfied them, since he had been home at the relevant hours, but Gavin, whose car had been seen dashing about the village late that night, had had to explain about visiting us, then taking Lois home, after which he had dropped his mother at their house, before going on with Sally to her home.

His mother had been in bed asleep when he had returned from Sally's, and since she had inadvertently told this to the police, it appeared that he had no witnesses to say how long had elapsed between the time when he left Sally and when he returned home.

Not that anyone genuinely suspected either Rory or Gavin of having had anything to do with the unfortunate woman's death, but when grandfather heard that the police had actually interrogated his nephew and step-son in connection with the murder, he became so excited that Phyllis had to send for Dr Menzies to give him something to calm him.

Aunt Morag too, had been flustered by the arrival of the police on her doorstep to interrogate her son, and had come to talk the matter over with Phyllis and Rory.

She was extremely anxious to know if Sergeant Dougal and the other officer had questioned Rory on similar lines to Gavin, and she kept cross-examining him about this and that and the next point as we sat in the sun lounge drinking afternoon tea.

Ever since the police visit, Rory had looked worried and had been very quiet and withdrawn, and even now, his replies to Aunt Morag's probings were terse and brusque and non-committal, and I could see she was beginning to get annoyed with him for not being more forthcoming.

Rory was becoming equally fed up with her searching quiz. He hastily finished his tea, and excused himself on the grounds that he had to tell MacPherson the gardener to cut back the creepers on the west wing wall, and he had better go and do so right away before the old man started on another job.

Aunt Morag's eyes followed him as he left the room.

"Rory doesn't seem to be himself today, Phyllis. What is the matter with him?" She looked at Rory's mother archly. "He wasn't by any chance one of that Molly creature's many young men?"

she sniffed. "From what I heard from my home help this morning, that young woman deserved what she got. She was unfaithful to her husband on more than one occasion."

Phyllis raised reproving eyebrows.

"Surely not? And in any case," she went on coldly, "the idea of Rory having anything to do with a married woman is quite ridiculous. He has too much good sense to involve himself with another man's wife, even if she was his type, which, from all accounts, poor Molly most certainly was not!"

Wickedly I intervened.

"Didn't Gavin take an interest in Molly at one time?"

"He was just a boy at the time," said Morag quickly. "And Molly was very young too, and unmarried."

She sighed. "I shall never know what he saw in her. She was pretty, I suppose, and rather appealing in a chocolate box way, but not in the least intelligent, and a man like Gavin needs a stimulating companion. Someone with his own background."

I tried to hide a smile. Aunt Morag is the snob of the family, with a terrific interest in family trees. She knew who begat who and who married who in the Conynghame family for generations back, and there had been times in the past, after grandmother's death, and before grandfather had married again, when she had assumed the role of lady of the manor, in spite of my mother's presence.

Phyllis glanced at her watch. "It is time that I gave Hugh his pills," she said, "and I feel I must sit with him quietly for a little. You don't mind if I leave you, do you Morag?"

"Of course not," said my aunt graciously. "Joanna has been home for almost a week, and would you believe it, we have not had a private chat together yet!"

Private inquisition would be more like it, I thought, and I said hurriedly:

"Actually, I was on my way to see if Rory would like a game of tennis, now that the rain has cleared away."

"You can play tennis with Rory any time," said Morag sharply. "This is my first opportunity—"

Before she could say any more, Rory returned to the room.

"Joanna," he addressed me. "I have been talking to Sergeant Dougal on the telephone. He would like to see you at the police station, and I said that I would take you there right away."

"What do the police want with Joanna?" asked Aunt Morag inquisitively.

"Sergeant Dougal did not say," replied Rory blandly, and my aunt looked peeved.

"I suppose you had better not keep the law waiting," she sniffed, and followed us from the room, "so I shall just have to go home. Say goodbye to Phyllis for me, and tell her to give me a ring tonight to let me know how Hugh is keeping, and if she still feels up to having the committee at Tarris tonight. If she doesn't, we can always arrange to have it at my house."

She got into Gavin's Jaguar, which she had borrowed for the afternoon, and drove off down the driveway, with almost as much verve as the girl she hoped would be her daughter-in-law, and Rory looked at the fast disappearing car and remarked:

"Morag Conynghame is a most amazing woman, isn't she? Do you know, that since she has come back to settle in Tarrisdale, which is not so very long ago, after all, she has already taken over the running of the Hospital Board, the Red Cross, the local Floral Art Club, and is even rumoured to be canvassing to be nominated as a Councillor at the next local elections!"

"I can believe it!" I assured him. "Aunt Morag always loved bossing the show. I don't think she has ever got over being an officer in the A.T.S. during the war!" I said with a laugh. "That was where she learned to drive, and Gavin's father used to say it showed, because she drove the family car as if it was an Army lorry!"

Rory grinned. "Yes. I have heard your grandfather say she must have made life a misery for the girls who served under her in the A.T.S. Everything has to be done her way, and like her son, she gives me the impression that she would not let much stop her if she wanted something badly."

He shook his head. "She was not at all pleased

when I deprived her of your company now, was she?"

"I was!" I smiled. "You have no idea how pleased I was to hear you calling me, even if it was only to drag me off to the police station!"

Rory returned my smile.

"Never mind. I shall see that they don't keep you there!" he promised.

Our eyes held, and as we stood there, smiling at each other, there came the knowledge which made me feel quite weak at the knees, that the reason why last night I could not have cared less when Gavin said he was going to see Lois, the reason I had been so resentful because Rory had gone off with him, and the reason, why, when I was with Rory, I felt so sensitively aware of his nearness.

For the first time in my life I was falling in love, and in love with a man who was interested in someone else.

With an effort I looked away from him, and was very pleased with the lightness I managed to get into my voice as I said:

"I shall hold you to that promise, Rory. Shall we put it to the test?"

He nodded, and we got into his car and drove down to Tarrisdale.

Chapter Twenty-One

I was glad that it took us only a few minutes to arrive at the police station.

The new found awareness of my feelings for Rory made me awkward and ill at ease with him. I was afraid that in an unguarded moment I might betray my emotions and this I was determined not to do.

It would probably amuse Rory no end to think that the girl who had snubbed his mother for marrying her grandfather should have fallen for his charm!

When we stopped in front of the two-storeyed, white-washed building, I turned to him and said curtly:

"Thanks for driving me here, Rory, but you don't need to wait for me. I think I shall visit the Misses Halbert after the police have finished with me, and I can get a bus home."

"No need for that," said Rory, easing himself out of the driving seat. "As it happens, I also want to have a word with Sergeant Dougal, and after that, well," he smiled at me with the smile which sent my pulses racing, "I am sure the Misses Halbert would not mind in the least if I visited them along with you. Just think of the gossip they will make out of it!" he went on teasingly.

I had to turn quickly away from him to hide the rising colour in my cheeks, and I was glad that after the bright sunshine which flooded the village street, inside the low-ceilinged hall of the police station it was shadowy and gloomy enough to tone down my betraying blush.

Rory followed close on my heels as I approached the desk where a young constable was busily making entries in a notebook, but before I could address the lad to tell him my business, Sergeant Dougal, who must have been on the look out for me, appeared from the private office on the right hand side of the corridor and came towards me.

"Ah! Miss Fraser!" he greeted me. "How good of you to come so promptly." He ushered me towards his office. "I hope I have not spoiled your plans for the afternoon," he went on, "and I promise I shall not keep you any longer than need be."

As I entered the room he turned to Rory.

"I don't expect we shall be more than ten minutes or so," he told him. "If you wish to wait for Miss Fraser, there is a chair over there by the desk," he indicated the wooden bench.

"I should like to have a word with you myself, Sergeant?" said Rory.

Dougal eyed him narrowly.

"I am very busy at the moment," he began, but Rory interrupted him.

"I have an idea that you will find what I have to say of interest to you," he promised. "I don't think I shall be wasting your time."

"Very well," conceded Dougal. "As I have

said, I don't expect to detain Miss Fraser more than a few minutes."

Rory went over to the bench, and the Sergeant followed me into his office and closed the door.

There were already two other men seated in the room. They rose as I entered and Sergeant Dougal introduced me to them. The uniformed Inspector was called Brown, and the other, heavier, man in plain clothes was a Detective Sergeant Colt.

The Inspector assumed charge of the interrogation.

"I expect you know, Miss Fraser," he began, "that we are not at all satisfied about the reason for Mrs Mackay's murder, and that we have already questioned everyone in this area who knew her?"

I nodded.

"So far we have learned nothing very helpful from our enquiries," he continued, "and also, we cannot dismiss the idea that an outsider might be involved."

He paused to offer me a cigarette, which I refused.

"We have been told that a stranger was seen in the Mackay cottage a few days ago. This man has been described as being of about medium height and build, with dark hair, an unpleasant face, and protruding eyes. Does such a description mean anything to you?"

I shook my head. "Medium height and build could cover a lot of people, but the protruding eyes, no, I am afraid I know of no one who would fit that detail."

"Our informant had never seen him before in Tarrisdale either," nodded the Inspector, "but are you quite sure this man means nothing to you?" He handed me a pencil sketch.

I studied the drawing, but the face was the face of a stranger.

"I am sorry, Inspector." Once more I shook my head.

Inspector Brown lifted up a sheaf of papers from the desk, and read from the top one.

"He was about medium height, I think, and neither fat nor thin, although it was difficult to judge his build because of the bulky jersey he wore. He had dark hair, and was very spry on his feet and—"

"Oh!" I interrupted him. "I see! You think this man could have been the man who was driving the stolen lorry!"

Brown nodded. "There is a marked similarity in the descriptions, which makes us think that the man you saw jump down from the lorry and the man seen at the Mackay's cottage could be one and the same person!"

"So Molly had another string to her bow after all! A man who must have resented the fact that she was also having an affair with Brook, and who tried to break up this relationship by getting Brook into trouble by stealing his lorry! When Molly found out what he had done, they had a quarrel and—" I stopped abruptly, remembering what the outcome of this quarrel must have been.

The Inspector was not to be drawn by my deduction.

"Are you sure you cannot add to your original description?" He looked at me hopefully.

I bit my lip thoughtfully.

In my mind's eye I replayed the dramatic scene of the few minutes before the crash the previous Friday. I could see the lorry as it came out of the layby and chugged up the steep hill in front of me. I could remember my impatience as it got slower and slower, until I had to change down to first gear. I could still almost smell the noxious exhaust fumes which set up a kind of smoke screen between me and the great lumbering vehicle, and I even remembered coughing to clear my throat of the acrid taste of burnt petrol at the very moment when the unbelievable happened, and the lorry door had been flung open, and the driver had jumped down from his cabin and gone scurrying over the brow of the hill, a crouching, dark-haired ball of humanity dressed in nondescript black trousers and a bulky pullover which distorted his physique so that he could have been fat or slim, young or old—no—surely not all that old, judging from the way he ran?

I frowned. Yes. There was something! A memory surfaced and vanished almost in the same instant.

"Have you remembered something else?"

asked the Inspector eagerly noting my change of expression.

"N-no!" I stammered. "I was merely thinking that the fellow was so smart on his feet, he must either be very young or in good training." I shook my head. "Apart from that, I am afraid I can add nothing to my original description. I truly am sorry I cannot help you more."

"So are we, Miss Fraser," said Brown. "Still it is not all that important. The description of the man seen at the Mackay's is quite a good one, and our informant also tells us that she feels she could identify him if she saw him again. We were really hoping to clear up two cases at the one go by asking you to confirm if the two descriptions tallied."

He stood up. "Thank you for coming along this afternoon, Miss Fraser. If we should need you again, I take it you will be staying at Tarris for some time?"

"Only another week," I told him. "Then I return to Edinburgh. Would you like my address there?"

He made a note of it, and Sergeant Dougal moved towards the door and opened it.

Rory was talking to the constable at the desk when I came out of the room.

He turned and came towards me.

"How did it go?" he asked.

"I wasn't much help, I'm afraid," I began, but Sergeant Dougal interrupted me.

"The Inspector can see you now, Mr Armstrong," he said. "He has not very much time."

Rory excused himself, and now it was my turn to sit and wait in the cool, antiseptic smelling hall of the police station.

As I moved uncomfortably on the hard, wooden bench, I kept thinking over my interview with Inspector Brown, and with natural curiosity, I wondered who the woman was who had visited Molly in her remote cottage, and had had such a good look at the man with the protuberant eyes. Molly must have been furious with her for arriving at such an inopportune moment, and the man must have been equally annoyed.

It was funny, but when the police had first mentioned an informant, I had immediately thought of Holy Willie, and I wondered if the police had also questioned him about this new suspect. It was more than likely that the old man knew what had been going on at the cottage, though why, with his religious mania, he had not denounced Molly publicly for the way she was deceiving her husband not once, but twice, I would never understand.

From behind the closed door of the private office I heard the murmur of voices. What was it that Rory had been so anxious to discuss with the police?

Rory.

Merely thinking of him gave me a tremulous sensation, and my eyes stared hopefully towards the door behind which he was hidden, willing him to come out soon.

I heaved a sigh. Really, it was preposterous that after knowing a man for such a short time he should affect me in this way. I had believed myself in love a half dozen times or so in the past years. The emotion I had felt then had been pleasant but evanescent. What I was feeling now was quite different.

It was as if Rory was someone I had unconsciously been looking for all my life; someone I had known all my life; someone to whom it was inevitable that I should be attracted.

I merely had to close my eyes and I could picture him as clearly as if he was standing in front of me, his hazel eyes twinkling, the tiny scar at the corner of his left lid white against the brown of his tanned skin, his mouth ready to widen to its humorous smile, or tighten with characteristic firmness when he was in one of his masterful moods. I could almost even hear the different tones of his expressive voice, and the infectious gaiety of his laugh.

I felt warm and glowing inside at the very thought of him, and for a few moments longer I kept my eyes closed to continue to savour the precious emotion.

The rustling of papers on the reception desk brought me back to reality, and quickly I opened my eyes again and heaved a sigh.

For my own peace of mind, I really should avoid being with Rory. For the rest of my stay in Tarrisdale I would make a point of not being around when he was.

This would not be too difficult. I could sit with grandfather each morning as I had been doing. In the afternoon I would go to visit old friends in the district, and at night, well, doubtless he would be out with Sally.

The remaining seven days of my visit would soon pass, and in future, when I revisited grandfather, I would find out beforehand if Rory was expected home.

I was bleakly studying the notices pinned on the board above the bench on which I was seated when Rory re-emerged from the private office, followed by Inspector Brown.

In spite of all my efforts, my pulses went racing madly as Rory glanced in my direction.

I rose to my feet, and said with forced lightness:

"I was beginning to think that the Inspector was detaining you as a suspicious character, Rory!"

There was no answering smile in the Inspector's eyes as he replied gravely:

"Miss Fraser, for your own good, it might be as well if you regarded anyone who in the least resembles the man I described to you a short time ago as a suspicious character."

I shot him a surprised look.

"I mean that," he said steadily. "And until we lay hands on the man who killed Mrs Mackay, I advise you not to wander off anywhere on your own." He cleared his throat gruffly. "We don't want another victim on our hands!"

I gaped at him, lips parted in amazement.

"What on earth do you mean? Surely you don't think the man can possibly still be in Tarrisdale, or that I should be in any danger from him! After what happened, a stranger here would be as noticeable as a man with a wooden leg!"

"From what Mr Armstrong has been saying, I am now wondering if the man is quite such a stranger to these parts," said the Inspector gravely. "In fact, we have come to the conclusion he is someone who knows his way round Tarrisdale extremely well. He could either be someone who comes here regularly on business or on holiday. After all," he pointed out, "if he had not visited Tarrisdale regularly, how could he possibly have got to know Molly Mackay? From what I have learnt of her, she has rarely been away from the village, and certainly never since she married Mackay."

"Which makes it all the more obvious why the man should stay away from here!" I decided.

"Staying away might be equally unwise, if his visits were regular," countered the policeman. "His absence could provoke as much suspicion as his presence, and he would know it! No, I doubt if he will stay away. He seems too wily a bird for that. Consider how no one, not even Mrs Mackay's very curious neighbor, Holy Willie, whom we have already questioned, ever guessed at his association with the dead woman!"

His lips tightened. "It is because he has been so keen to cover up his connection with Mrs Mackay that we are particularly urging both you and Miss Burgess to be on the look out. You are the only two who might connect him with her, and having killed once, he has nothing to lose by killing again to keep his secret!"

"Miss Burgess?" I repeated the name he had mentioned. "I did not realize that she was your other witness."

"Didn't I mention that it was she who saw him when she called at the Mackay house a week ago about rent arrears?"

I shook my head.

"Poor Lois. She was upset enough over seeing Molly's body without having this hanging over her."

"You worry about yourself, not Lois!" said Rory firmly. "She has her father to keep an eye on her, and she has plenty of common sense not to wander off anywhere on her own. She will be perfectly safe."

He was wrong there.

There was a final meeting of the Fête committee at Tarris House that evening. Sally had to leave early because the woman who was sitting in with her mother had to leave at ten o'clock, and Gavin took her home in the Land Rover. Then, when the meeting eventually broke up, Mrs Conynghame drove Lois home in the Jaguar, after a slight altercation as to who should drive.

She dropped the girl outside her gate and drove off while Lois proceeded to the front door of her house along the dark, shadowy path bordered on either side by a thick unkempt shrubbery.

Seconds before she reached the front door,

someone leapt out on her from the densely packed bushes.

She screamed and struggled. Fortunately her father heard her cries. His timely arrival chased off her assailant, but not before he had half strangled her with the long, dangling chain pendant she had been wearing round her neck.

Chapter Twenty-two

News of the attack on Lois was kept from grandfather although it was the chief topic of conversation on everyone else's lips, and by the time I had heard everyone's opinion of the affair, if it hadn't been for grandfather, I think I would have followed their advice and taken the coward's way out and left Tarrisdale forthwith.

As for my hopeful resolution to avoid seeing any more of Rory than I need, this proved impossible. For two days he trailed around with me wherever I went, as if he was afraid that something would happen to me if he let me out of his sight. He joined me in my morning visits to grandfather; he accompanied me when I went on my visits to friends in the afternoon, and in the evenings we played tennis or scrabble together. I could not even enjoy this bitter sweet relationship, in case I gave myself away, and yet, when I went to bed at night, I would go nostalgically over the minutes of our hours together in my mind.

Rory's devotion and constant companionship

naturally set the local tongues wagging. I was aware that we were the cynosure of all eyes as we walked through the village together, and I could not help feeling sorry for poor Sally, who must have thought I had superseded her in Rory's affections.

There was one person who was openly delighted at the way Rory continually squired me, and this was grandfather. On the one occasion when Rory happened to leave us alone together, he confided to me that he had rather hoped that Rory and I might make a match of it, and this made me feel worse than ever, for I could not explain to him that Rory was cherishing me out of a sense of duty, and not for the reason he thought.

In fact, with one thing and another, I was beginning to feel the strain of my position. The more I was with Rory, the more difficult it was for me to hide my feelings for him under a cloak of casual friendship.

I even began to wish that he would be recalled to duty because of some emergency, and yet, when on the third day after the attack on Lois he knocked on my bedroom door at six o'clock in the morning and called to suggest that it would be an ideal day to carry out the assault on Ben Nevis which we had once discussed, I felt quite light headed at the thought of spending an entire day with him, with no one else around to catch me out should my guard slip, as it had been in danger of doing several times in the past forty-eight hours.

"I shall go and make some sandwiches and fill a flask with coffee while you are getting dressed," he called softly when I told him that I should be delighted to attempt the climb.

I put on slacks and a silk blouse, with a thickish sweater on top, and tied my hair back from my forehead with a green velvet ribbon which matched the green of the sweater. I put on thick socks and my "sensible" shoes to guard my feet against the flinty ruggedness of the mountain tracks, and hurried down to the kitchen.

Rory eyed my outfit with approval as he said:

"I have pushed a note under mother's door and told her where we are going. I said we should be back in time for dinner."

The Lotus was the only car on the road as we went speeding through Tarrisdale, but a couple of milk floats were already out on their rounds and several fishermen were down at their boats in the harbour.

As we made our way over the Pass of Tarris and out of the deep shadows of its gully, I felt a tremendous relief, as if I was leaving behind me a world of fear and suspicion.

Ahead of us lay a long, empty stretch of sunlit road, on either side of which rose beautiful, sun dappled mountains, magnificent in their multicoloured coverings of pale green bracken and deep pine forest, purple heather and plum tinted scree. Calm-eyed sheep, munching contentedly at the grass of the verges, looked up at us with their steady gaze, and the whole world seemed a place of utter peace.

"Wouldn't it be wonderful to go driving on and on, to the world's end on a day like this!" I sighed.

Rory glanced at me.

"Ultima Thule rather than Ben Nevis?"

I nodded.

"I am an escapist, I am afraid."

"I wouldn't say that," he said firmly. "It has not been much fun for you this past couple of days, and I think you have borne up nobly."

"Lois has been pretty noble too." I wanted to get away from speaking about myself. "Fancy going out and about the way she does after what happened to her! If she didn't have to wear a scarf to cover the marks on her throat, you could almost think she had dreamed up the whole episode."

"Lois is a pretty strong minded character," said Rory. "The success she had in her work in London proves that. And don't forget," he continued, "she is never without an escort when she goes about her business. I think she rather enjoys being squired round by the handsome Police Inspector or his equally handsome Sergeant. Indeed," he remarked dryly, "I never knew policemen to take their work so seriously. I wonder what Gavin thinks about them?"

I was not particularly interested in what Gavin thought, and in any case talk of crime and police escorts was talk which reminded me of the unpleasantness I wanted to forget for today, so I deliberately changed the subject.

"How long do you think it will take us to get to the top of the Ben?" I asked.

He gave me a keen, speculative glance before replying.

"That depends which path we go by, and what condition you are in!"

"I have not done any serious hill walking or rock climbing for the past five years, so we should be wiser to stick to the easiest route," I suggested. "In any case, I am not trying to prove anything to myself by reaching the top. I merely want the satisfaction of getting there."

"Good!" he smiled. "We can take it easy then and have time to enjoy all the splendid views, and you will enjoy them, Joanna," he assured me. "I know you will."

From Fort William it is not easy to get a really good view of the highest mountain of the British Isles. The base of the ben is so broad, reckoned to be about twenty-four miles in circumference, and the surrounding mountains so close, that with its summit invariably hidden in clouds, it is difficult to distinguish it from its neighbours.

We drank a coffee at a transport café on the outskirts of the little town to refresh ourselves before we set off on the first stages of the climb, up the glen and along past a white farmhouse.

The sun was warm on our shoulders and its strong light accentuated the brilliant colours of the mountain, the green of the grasses, the golden flourish of gorse, the silver of the ladylike birches, the rich deep greens of fir and pine, the deepening purple haze of the early bell heather and the variegated damsons and pinks and cobalts and greys of the rock faces.

There was no one else to be seen as we trudged past little spinneys and patches of heather moorland and bogs where the white cotton grass tossed like a drift of candy floss on the breeze.

The only sounds were the clatter of our feet on the flinty path, the occasional bleat of a sheep as it moved away from us into the heather by the side of the track, the busy chatter of the clear stream which tumbled down from the high slopes and the sweet call of the larks which soared in the blue sky overhead.

After a time, Rory paused to let me have a rest.

I had not realized how far we had come. From where we now stood, the farmhouse we had passed near the base seemed almost match box size, and the far away roadways seemed narrow as the ribbon I wore in my hair.

I felt quite remote from the world, as if I were now a being from another planet. I sighed blissfully and turned to Rory, whose eyes were directed not downwards, but up to the summit of the great mountain, where gauzy clouds veiled, but did not completely obscure, the final yards of our climb.

I sat down on a rock and watched him, absorbed by the changing expressions on his face.

After a few minutes he turned to me.

"Are you ready to go on now, Joanna?" he asked.

I nodded.

"It is not quite such an easy climb from here on," he warned, "and it could get much cooler. I would advise you to put your jersey on again."

I obeyed him like an obedient child.

We climbed more slowly now. The path became more rugged; the flints sharper underfoot; the rocks seemed to encroach more awesomely.

We were now above the lesser mountains, and passing a lovely gem of a loch which sparkled like a sapphire with the blue reflection of the summer sky.

The air grew colder, the path steeper still, and each time I paused for breath, and to look behind me, another even more magnificent scene was revealed. I caught a glimpse of the Atlantic and the dim, mysterious outlines of the further western isles.

I was hot, and tiring, but enjoying every step we took, when at length we reached the summit and Scotland lay below us.

Now I felt the most glorious sense of exhilaration and exaltation. I was so moved by the scene that I turned to Rory, eyes alight with happiness, mouth parted in a smile, and in a physical expression of my mood, I stepped forward and gave him an impetuous hug.

Chapter Twenty-three

Rory's arms instinctively tightened round me. He bent his head and kissed me on the lips with growing intensity.

I responded momentarily to his caress, but the clattering of the boots on the flinty path a few yards below us fortunately brought me to my senses before I made a fool of myself.

Rory had reacted to my embrace as any normal, warm-blooded male would have done, but I had very nearly betrayed my own deeper feelings by my response to him.

I felt weak at the knees and ashamed of my weakness. Somehow I managed to pull myself away from his embracing arms, and with a laugh whose apparent spontaneity would have earned high praise from a drama critic, I murmured:

"I am sorry, Rory! I hope I haven't embarrassed you with my enthusiasm, but I did want to say a nice 'Thank you' to my favourite step-uncle for today's treat!"

I retreated another couple of steps, hoping that my legs would not give way before I managed to sit down on a convenient boulder.

An odd expression flitted across Rory's face as he watched me, and there was a lack of the usual bantering tone in his voice as he replied abruptly:

"I am afraid that I am not used to playing

step-uncle to a pretty girl, Joanna. Please forgive me."

The sun went behind a cloud, but it was not the sudden chill from the exclusion of sunlight, or the icy whirl of gusting winds whipping my jersey tight against my body which made me feel cold to the very marrow of my bones. Rather was it the sense of utter desolation I felt because Rory sounded as if he despised me as a flirt who gave her kisses lightly, and there was nothing I could say in my defence.

The arrival of another party of climbers broke the awkward silence between us, and I was glad when Rory asked if we could join up with them, when they made the descent.

Even as we drove back to Tarrisdale, there was constraint between us, and when we spoke, it was as polite strangers.

All through dinner that night Phyllis watched us with a worried frown, and aware of the question she must be trying to formulate, after we had taken our after dinner coffee in front of the log fire in the hall, on the excuse of being completely tired out after the day's outing, I asked to be excused so that I could get to bed early.

"What a pity you have to be up so early tomorrow again, to help with the preparations for the Fête," said Phyllis. "If Hugh had not insisted that it be held in the grounds of Tarris as usual this year, we could have excused ourselves from a lot of extra work. As it is," she said with a sigh, "the men are coming with the tents and marquees at eight o'clock, and although I have the treasure hunt all arranged, the side shows have still to be marked out and the catering arrangements seen to."

She stood up. "Thank goodness the lawn we are using is out of sight of the house, or Hugh would get excited just watching what was going on."

"I shall get up as early as possible, and give you all the help I can, Phyllis," I promised. "In any case, I should not worry too much about it. I don't suppose that after coping with it for five years, I need to tell you that as an institution, the Fête has gone on for so many years that it practically runs itself!"

"Aunt Morag will throw her weight about too!" Rory was beginning to sound more like his usual cheerful self. "There is a born organizer for you! She knows exactly what she wants and how she wants it done, and woe betide the helpers who don't jump to attention at her command!"

He grinned suddenly. "I can see a few arguments between her and Lois in the future, with Gavin torn between them!"

"Gavin is every bit as strong minded as either Lois or Morag," I retorted. "The only thing is that he gets what he wants more subtly!"

With that, I stood up and crossed the hall with Phyllis to go to grandfather's room for our usual few minutes chat before bedtime. When I returned to go to my room, Rory had left the hall, without even waiting to bid me goodnight, and I trailed upstairs with the feeling that I was still in his black books.

I was both physically and emotionally tired that night and I slept from the moment I slipped between the lavender smelling linen sheets of my bed, until my little alarm clock roused me at seven o'clock the following morning.

I got up and drew the bedroom curtains and was delighted to see the sun streaming down from a not too cloudy sky.

It was breezy and there were white horses prancing across Loch Tarris and puffy white clouds chasing each other gaily across the summer sky. From my knowledge of local weather I realized that the chances of rain during the day were slight, although it might come on later in the evening, and that Tarrisdale Fête was going to continue to enjoy its unbroken tradition of always taking place on a good day.

I dressed quickly, but early as I was, Phyllis and Rory were already in the breakfast-room when I came downstairs.

We all went in to see grandfather before going off to perform our allotted chores in connection with the Fête.

Grandfather was looking brighter than I had seen him look for the past couple of days, and once or twice I caught him glancing quizzically from Rory to me.

I wondered if Phyllis had said anything to him about our coolness to each other the previous evening, and because I did not want him to be upset again by what might appear to be another family quarrel, I forced myself to treat Rory in our usual friendly, teasing fashion.

Mrs. Conynghame, Lois, Gavin and Sally came up together shortly after nine o'clock, and by twelve noon, everything was ready for the official opening at two o'clock.

With all the excitement of the preparations that morning, I had forgotten about Inspector Brown's warning of possible danger to me, but I was reminded of this less happy aspect of things after lunch, when the Inspector arrived at Tarris accompanied by Sergeant Dougal and Detective Sergeant Colt, followed a few minutes later by another carload of plain clothes men.

"We thought we would come along and keep an eye on things," said Brown, his sharp eyes wandering round the garden as if he suspected some felon was hiding behind every bush. "I don't like crowds. They make things difficult for us, so be sure and watch out for yourself, Miss Fraser. Don't give our man a chance to get up to more mischief!"

"I shall get Sergeant Colt to watch out for me!" said Lois, gaily commandeering the handsome detective as her personal bodyguard. "He can collect the money outside the fortune teller's tent for me, and in that way he will be doing a useful job for charity as well as screening my callers."

My particular side-show, for those hopefuls who wanted to win silver coins set under bottles, by dropping a curtain ring over the long-necked flagons, was set out between Rory's shooting gallery and the cake and candy stall, on the outer perimeter of the lawn, hard up against the shrubbery.

By quarter to two, the garden was a seething mass of people and parking places in the driveway and in every available space between the trees in the adjoining copse, and along one side of the main road from the gateway, were all used up.

Constable McGregor, his face crimson with the strong sun and his impatience at drivers who would not obey his signals, directed traffic along the main road, and he must have envied his colleagues whose work keeping an eye on Lois and myself would seem so much easier and cooler than his.

Outside the refreshment marquee a wooden platform had been erected, and just before two o'clock the platform party arrived to take their seats.

Lord Mantonairlie, the Lord Lieutenant of the county and his wife sat beside Lady Carnwallis, an old friend of grandfather's who had come up from Surrey to perform the opening ceremony. Phyllis, looking extremely attractive in a rose pink linen suit with a fine straw, broad brimmed black hat, sat beside Mantonairlie and next to her was General Marchsides, whose estate borders Tarris, and his wife.

Gavin sat between Amelia Mantonairlie and his mother, and the M.P. for the area was the other member of the platform party.

The press was out in full force, with representatives from as far away as Inverness and Dundee. The Tarrisdale Garden Fête is famous not only locally, but nationally, because it attracts house parties from many of the famous estates in the Highlands, and is not infrequently patronized by members of the Royal family.

Aunt Morag was in her element, bowing graciously to acquaintances with her naturally assumed 'grande dame' manner, and I shot Rory an amused look as we stood with Sally and Lois and Sergeant Colt on the fringe of the crowd which surrounded the platform.

He gave me an answering grin, and the amused twinkle he shot me was noticed by Sally, who turned sharply to look at me, and I hastily averted my gaze.

Rory himself might be ignorant of my true feelings for him, but a woman in love with him would be more perceptive, and I did not want to give Sally Henderson cause for unease.

When the speeches were over and Lady Carnwallis had been duly presented with her bouquet of exquisite white carnations, which are a speciality of the Tarris glasshouses, those of us in charge of stalls had to hurry off to take up our positions.

Unfortunately because Lois wanted to see the final presentation, we found we had left our leave taking rather late, and we were hemmed in by the crowd as people started the rush for the stalls.

In the press of bodies I was forced tightly against Rory's stalwart frame. He put a protective arm around me and held me close to him. Our physical contact made my bones feel wobbly as aspic, and I tried to wriggle away.

At that moment something pointed and painful prodded into my back below my left shoulder blade and I let out an involuntary scream.

Chapter Twenty-four

At my startled cry, Rory grabbed me even tighter, and Sergeant Colt caught hold of Lois and pushed her between Sally and himself for protection.

"Damn!" exclaimed Gavin, his face scarlet with mortification as he stood beside me. "I didn't mean to give you a fright, Joanna. I just meant to give you a gentle prod, but someone bumped into my arm and shoved me forward."

I gave a shaky laugh.

"I have never known a finger feel as sharp as the point of a knife before!" I was trembling. "That shows what a vivid imagination I have!"

"You stupid idiot!" Rory's face was dark with anger. "You know the strain Joanna is under." He continued to hold me close, as though he wanted to impart some of his own strength into my wobbly limbs.

"I have already said I am sorry," said Gavin stiffly. "Joanna is the last person I would want to upset. You know that, don't you, Joanna?" He turned to me, his eyes pleading forgiveness.

"We are all on edge." My voice was still shaking. "Let's forget about it, shall we?"

"What is all the fuss about?"

Aunt Morag came ploughing through the crowd, which parted before her as water parts before the prow of a battleship. "Why are you not at your stalls? We shall be losing money if we don't get started right away."

The normality of her tone was what we all needed to settle us, and with a gruff, "I shall arrange to see you later, Joanna," Gavin went off to start the treasure hunt, and Lois departed to her tent to change into her gypsy costume for her afternoon's session as a fortune teller and crystal gazer.

Sally dutifully followed Aunt Morag to the cake and candy stall, and I found myself, still clinging to Rory's hand, being masterfully led to my own side show.

When we reached our stance, Rory eyed me keenly.

"You still look pretty white about the gills, Joanna. I could keep an eye on both stalls, if you want to go back to the house and sit quietly with your grandfather. I am sure he would enjoy your company this afternoon, when everyone else is otherwise engaged."

I took a deep breath.

"I am all right now, thanks, Rory."

Reluctantly I withdrew my hand from his. "If I went back to the house now, and sat with grandfather, he might start worrying that he was not well enough to be left on his own, and that would not be wise, would it?"

"In that case," he smiled warmly at me, "perhaps you should stick to your post, but if you need me, remember, I am right here beside you, keeping an eye on you!"

He gave my arm an affectionate squeeze and went off to attend to the queue of youngsters and local crackshots who were lining up to try their luck at his rifle range.

My stall appealed more to school children, and was never quite as busy as Rory's, and also drew far less of a crowd than Aunt Morag's cake and candy stall, which as usual was going to prove the biggest money earner of the afternoon.

Although the Fête closed at four thirty, there was a lot of tidying up to be done after the last member of the public left. Fortunately it was such a long established institution, and every one of the helpers was geared to his or her particular job, so that by seven o'clock, except for the churned up state of the grass, the grounds were almost as they had been forty-eight hours previously.

Phyllis looked rather jaded when the last of the lorries rolled off down the drive with the tent equipment, but Aunt Morag was as zestful as ever, and looking forward to attending the Barn Dance in the village hall, which was the usual way of rounding off Fête day.

I was not very keen to go but Aunt Morag was persistent.

"It would look odd if you did not join our

party, Joanna," she declared. "You know that everyone who has anything to do with the Fête goes."

"If I go with you, it will make the numbers uneven," I pointed out.

"Rubbish! There are always unattached males at the dance, and I expect Sergeant Colt will be there, keeping an eye on you, so we can get him to make up the numbers. I am sure he won't object."

"Of course you must go!" Phyllis added her voice to the argument. "Your grandfather will want to hear all about it at first hand tomorrow.

"It is so long since I have danced 'The Gay Gordon' and 'Strip the Willow' or even taken part in an eightsome reel, that I would be an encumbrance to a partner." I was still not eager to go.

"There are modern dances now as well," said Lois. "Our local beat group is quite famous, and worth listening to even if you don't want to dance. Yes. You must come."

"Of course you must." Sally smiled at me. "You are here on holiday, remember?"

"We shall all meet at my house at nine o'clock," said Aunt Morag. "That gives us plenty of time to dine and change."

It would have been churlish of me to argue further, but as I went up to my room to change from the tired looking clothes I had been wearing that afternoon, I wished I had had the courage to abide by my original refusal. I knew I was going to spend a miserable evening watching Sally dancing contentedly in Rory's arms, and at the thought of him smiling down at her with love in his glance, two great tears welled from the corners of my eyes and spilled on to the polished wood of the dressing table.

If Rory had to prefer blondes, why Sally rather than me?

I put on the same gay dress I had worn my first evening at Tarris, and the same silly golden sandals.

Rory shook his head at this.

"You will never be able to dance an eightsome in these!" he protested.

"I shall sit and watch you," I replied.

"Nonsense!" said Phyllis, who had come to the door to see us off. "If you find your shoes uncomfortable for dancing in, do what I do, and dance bare-footed. You get much more of a spring in your reels that way."

I laughed, and Rory tucked his arm in mine and led me across the courtyard to where his car was standing.

The dance was fun, and even if I did not have a partner of my own, there were so many old friends and former playmates of my youth wanting to dance with me and hear about what I had been doing since I had left Tarrisdale, that the evening passed quickly and pleasantly.

I danced an eightsome with Gavin and a very gay "Gay Gordon" with Rory, and when the last dance was announced, Mr Burgess gallantly bowed to me and asked me for the honour, which I could hardly refuse him.

Aunt Morag, who considered him her official partner, looked furious, and immediately took Gavin's arm making it clear where his duty lay.

Sergeant Colt, beaming delightedly, commandeered Lois, and Rory and Sally went waltzing past me in each other's arms, laughing at some shared joke.

The music came to an end, and we joined hands in a circle to sing "Auld Lang Syne," before the final hectic rush to the cloakroom for wraps and coats.

I eventually managed to find my own scarlet linen coat, and push my way out to the car park at the back of the hall, where members of different parties were anxiously searching for each other.

I had no difficulty in finding my own party. Aunt Morag's voice had the carrying power of a fog horn, and she hailed each one of us in turn as we appeared, telling us that we were to go back to Lois's house for a coffee to round off the evening. Her invitation included Sergeant Colt, who accepted with alacrity and squeezed into the back seat of the Jaguar beside Lois.

Sally, who had also come in the Jaguar was about to get into the front seat beside Gavin and his mother, but because I did not want to be alone with Rory in his car, I smartly nipped into the Jaguar before her, in spite of Lois's sudden black look, and Sally perforce had to go with Rory in the Lotus, which would make them both happy.

If they were happy, for some reason, Gavin was not, and the speed with which he drove home, the way he skidded round corners making the tyres squeal emphasized his bad mood.

By the time we reached the Burgess's house, my nerves felt taut to snapping point, and after listening for half an hour to Aunt Morag's monologue about how the Fête should be run, I was grateful when Rory announced firmly that it was time he took me home.

This was a signal for the party to break up, and Mr Burgess happily rounded off his evening by helping Sally and I into our coats and bestowing a more than avuncular kiss on us as he said "Goodnight".

"Thank goodness that is over." I yawned sleepily as Rory and I drove off.

Rory grinned.

"You can say that again! Almost eighteen hours of listening to Morag Conynghame is asking a lot of human good nature!"

"Gavin was not in a particularly good mood, was he?" I snuggled back comfortably into my seat.

"He has something on his mind," Rory frowned. "I have thought that for several days."

He shot me a questioning glance, "What was it he was so anxious to discuss with you this afternoon?"

"I have no idea," I shook my head. "I had only one dance with him this evening, and an eightsome is not the kind of dance in which you can indulge in a private conversation!"

"You were very much in demand tonight, Joanna. I had not realized you were so well known locally. Do you realize that I had only one dance with you myself?" He shook his head. "You must think me remiss as a partner, particularly when I was foiled from giving you the last waltz."

I turned to him in surprise as we drew up outside the front door of Tarris House.

"I thought Sally was your partner!"

"Sally?" he raised his brows. "Why should she have been? She is a pleasant enough lass, and easy to talk to, but she is not the kind of girl who would attract me strongly. Not the kind of girl I could live with for ever and a day."

He laughed harshly as he switched off the engine.

"There is only one woman I have felt like that about. Only one," he repeated as he got out of the car and noisily slammed the door behind him.

I frowned as I too got out of the car.

Rory had not bothered to wait for me, but was already striding away towards the front steps.

I stared after him. Had I said something to offend him?

I ran up to him, and touched his arm as he pushed open the heavy oak front door.

"Rory! What is the matter? What have I said to upset you?"

He whirled round and looked down at me.

The light from the porch exaggerated the thickness of his beetling brows and the angry, scowling lines of his face.

"How you must be laughing at me, Joanna Fraser!" he rasped. "How you must be enjoying this moment!"

He seized me, his hands on my shoulders digging painfully through the fine linen of my scarlet summer coat and bruising the flesh beneath.

"I love you, Joanna. You. You, you aggravating, teasing, impossibly lovely witch!"

For the second time he forced his lips against mine. His kiss was hard, demanding, hurtful.

I longed to respond, but I was so faint with the shock of his profession of love that I could not do so. I started to weep with sheer happiness, and as the tears coursed down my cheeks, as abruptly as he had seized me, Rory pushed me away.

"My darling," he groaned. "I didn't mean to upset you. I am sorry!" He gave me a look of utter misery and then turned and went hurrying across the hall and up to his room.

I stood mutely staring after him, my fingers digging nervously into the shallow pocket of the coat I was wearing in an effort to regain control of myself.

Rory loved me! I repeated the wonderful news to myself, and as the first wave of shock passed, I wanted to cry out to him to wait for me, but the words would not come, and my legs were still too shaky to go racing after him.

Slowly I withdrew my hands from my pockets, and as I did so, I pulled out an envelope.

I looked at it with surprise. Where on earth had it come from? I never keep anything in my coat pockets. The envelope was sealed and unaddressed, and I decided that sometime during the evening, someone must have put it into my pocket for me to find.

I closed and locked the front door and went slowly up to my room, still holding the envelope in my hand.

I cast a loving glance across the well of the hall to Rory's room, which was opposite mine, before entering my room.

What a day this had been, I thought as I wearily sat down on the dressing table stool.

A tiring day. A trying day. A wonderful, wonderful day!

I wondered how I would face Rory in the morning. I knew my instinct would be to go right up to him and return the unfinished embrace.

I shivered with pleasure at the thought, as my fingers automatically ripped open the envelope I was still holding.

It contained a brief note from Gavin, a note which seemed to promise an explanation of his odd behaviour.

"Meet me at the Pulpit tomorrow, before I start work at nine," I read. "There is something I must talk over with you."

Chapter Twenty-five

Curiosity as to why Gavin wanted to see me so secretly was not so potent as my happiness at Rory's unexpected declaration of love.

I fell asleep with a smile on my lips, thinking of him and imagining what the morrow would be like when I told him that I returned his feelings.

I snuggled blissfully between the cool sheets at the thought.

When I woke up, it was almost eight o'clock and I jumped briskly out of bed. I did not want to be late for breakfast on this particular day.

I put on my slacks and the green jumper that Rory had admired, and brushed my hair until it gleamed.

Although there was a grey mist outside, blotting out sight of the loch and even part of the shrubbery, and a persistent light rain was falling, giving the landscape a dank, miserable look, I felt as if the sun was shining. I was so happy.

To my disappointment, Phyllis was alone in the breakfast-room.

"Good morning, my dear," she greeted me. "I did not expect you down so promptly this morning. Aren't you tired after dancing all night? Rory tells me you thoroughly enjoyed yourself."

"I certainly did!" I nodded. "And I slept like a top! I feel absolutely wonderful this morning!"

She smiled at my enthusiasm.

"How is grandfather this morning?" I asked

her. "I hope we didn't waken him when we came in last night?"

"He did have rather a restless night." The smile faded from her face. "In yesterday's general excitement I stupidly forgot to get more of his pills, but Rory has gone off to see if he can get some made up for him."

"It is a good job Mr Meeks lives above his chemist's shop, isn't it?" she went on. "He provides us with a twenty-four-hour service."

I tried not to let my spirits droop when I realized that I might not have a chance to see Rory before my rendezvous with Gavin, and I kept glancing out of the window to see if I could see his car coming up the drive.

I finished breakfast and went in to say "Good morning" to grandfather, but he had fallen asleep, and I crept out without waking him.

Phyllis went upstairs to give Mrs Oliver a hand with changing the bed linen, and I sat in the hall and half-heartedly glanced through a fashion magazine, hopefully waiting for Rory to return, and equally hopefully waiting for the telephone to ring and Gavin to tell me that in view of the miserable day, he wanted to postpone our meeting. Surely what he wanted to talk to me about could not be so desperately urgent that he expected me to trail through the sodden wood to the lonely "Pulpit" rock, in the bay at the far end of the estate, where it bordered the local cemetery.

The Pulpit is a peculiar rock formation, which on the seaward side looks rather like a great chair. It juts up about fifteen feet into the air from a sandy stretch of Seal Cove, a tiny crescent shaped bay between Tarris point and Tarrisdale harbour.

Because of its seclusion, the cove is a sort of local lovers' trysting place, and the "Pulpit" is decorated with innumerable initials and hearts.

Apart from its fame as a meeting place for courting couples, the bay is notorious for its fast rising tide, which is a result of the almost bottle-neck narrowness of its seaward entrance, and several times a lover and his lass have had to stay marooned for several hours on the highest point of the rock, while the water laps over the stone seat.

I waited until only a few minutes before nine in anticipation of his call, but when it did not come, I reluctantly pulled on a pair of wellington boots, and an old raincoat, tied a plastic hood over my hair, and went trudging off through the shrubbery and through the slippery, moss carpeted woods of lower Tarris, down to the rugged track which led to the rendezvous.

Water dripped from the pine branches and runnelled down the plastic of my hood to seep through the shoulders of my coat, and by the time I eventually came to the sandy shore, I was in an angry mood, and preparing to tell Gavin exactly what I thought of him for dragging me to this desolate spot on such a morning.

A trail of scuffed footprints on the sand leading to the solitary rocky pinnacle which stood near the water's edge, indicated that Gavin had arrived before me, but I could not see him, and guessed he was sheltering from the rain on the far side of the Pulpit, which looked hazy and insubstantial in the swirling, misty, drizzle.

As I struggled across the damp sand, my lips were already forming the words with which I would berate Gavin, and when I reached the rock, I opened my mouth to give vent to my indignation, but the words never came.

Something hard and stunning hit me forcefully across the forehead, and I went staggering down on my knees on the wet sand. Another vicious blow knocked me flat on the ground, and as consciousness began to drift away, I felt myself hauled roughly across the grit and propped up against the wall of rock on the seaward side.

"There, Joanna Fraser!" said a gloating voice. "See if the silver spoon you were born with can help you now!"

Painfully I opened my eyes, and saw Lois Burgess sneering down at me, the features I had once thought so lovely contorted into a grimace of such hate that I cringed back against the rock.

"What is it? What are you doing here? Where is Gavin?" I whimpered, trying to pull myself to my feet.

"I knew a note from Gavin would bring you running!" snarled Lois. "You wanted him as well as everything else, didn't you?"

I stared at her, appalled by her tone and her manner. I was dreaming, I told myself. I must be. That was why my head felt so light and peculiar. This reality could not be real! Why should Lois Burgess be standing over me with a murderous look in her eyes and a stocking filled with sand swinging like a truncheon from her hand?

As I shook my head to try to clear away the dizzy feeling, she bent down and smacked me savagely across the face.

"Yes, Joanna, you wanted him too, didn't you, and you tried to get him from me! Don't think I know nothing about those secret meetings you have had several nights this week! I have watched him come through the woods to meet you here, and I could have killed you then, only I knew he was merely amusing himself with you," she sneered. "Gavin has only two loves. Me, and Tarris. He might think that he puts Tarris first, and might marry you to possess it, but I would not let him do that!" her voice rose angrily.

"I am going to arrange it that he will have both his loves. Both me and Tarris. You see, I have it all planned. How to get rid of you and Sir Hugh at one go!"

Little flecks of saliva appeared at the corner of her mouth, and she licked her lips.

"Your death, by accident, would shock your grandfather to his, and then everything will come to Gavin, everything! The title, the estate, the money—and Gavin will be mine! It will all be mine!" her voice rose to a triumphant scream.

"I will not be poor Lois any longer. Poor Lois who could never get beyond the fringe; who always had to accept second best; who was never considered quite good enough for the circle I wanted to move in in London. But soon I shall be Lady Conynghame with plenty of money and a show place of a house, and I shall be the one in the middle of the Society photographs!"

My head swam with pain as Lois's voice kept going on and on, now loud, now soft, and her awful, mad looking face appeared and disappeared in front of my eyes as the waves of dizziness seized me.

"You are a hard person to kill, Joanna Fraser," her voice droned on. "I tried that first day when you returned to Tarrisdale. You see, months and months ago I learned that only you stood between me and the kind of life I had always dreamed of having, and I began to plan how I could get rid of you. Fate played into my hands. I heard you were coming back to Tarrisdale. I even learned the very hour of your arrival!

"There had been a fatal accident on the Tarris Pass the week I came back to live here. It was an accident which fascinated me. A lorry's brakes failed, and it rolled backwards and took a following car with it over the edge of the road, down into the gully, killing the occupants.

"I realized I could encompass your death in a similar way. I knew about Molly Mackay and Harry Brook, and how he left his lorry hidden near her house for hours on end. A rough track leads from the Mackays' house to the main road. It all seemed so easy. All I had to do was wait in the lorry till I saw your car coming, and re-enact the old accident!"

"Oh, no!" I gasped. "That couldn't have been you!" I stopped. But of course it had! Too late I remembered the something which had eluded me these past days. I had thought there was something odd about the way the lorry driver had run—like a woman's way of running—and when I had seen Lois run ahead of me down the path to the boathouse I had momentarily seen the resemblance, then forgotten about it almost instantly, because I had had other things on my mind.

Lois went on:

"I was unlucky that day. Not only did you escape without hurt from the accident, but that evening at dinner at Tarris I learned I might have been seen taking the lorry by Holy Willie. I had stupidly forgotten about him. I went to his house that night to silence him, but he had already been taken to hospital. Unluckily for her, Molly Mackay saw me prowling about his place at two in the morning, and asked me what I was up to. I dare not let her broadcast that she had seen me, so I had to get rid of her." Lois spoke without any emotion.

"She was very easy to kill, and I used Dr Menzies' car to dump her body in the loch. I knew that no one would look twice at the doctor's car if they saw it on the road late at night," she explained.

"I got a bit of a shock when I saw her body again in the fisherman's net at Abbess Inch, and I was sure I had given myself away that day, which is why I made up a cock and bull story of seeing a stranger in Molly's house one day. I staged that attack on myself to indicate that I too might be in danger from this man. Wasn't that clever of me?" she went on in her curious high-pitched voice.

I shuddered. "Lois, you are making all this up. You couldn't have killed Molly!"

"Do you think I could have let that silly little flibberty gibbet interfere with my plans?" She gave me a vicious look. "Molly was easy. You never were!

"I tried to get rid of you at other times. Remember the night you arrived at Tarris? When you were alone in the west wing, dressing for dinner, I sneaked back to the house, jammed the corridor door with a bead, so that you would have to use the outside entrance to get to the old wing, and I tied a strong thread across the second top step of the flight leading down to the path. I did not see how you could avoid tripping over it, and you were meant to go crashing through the railing to your death, but I did not have enough time to weaken the base of the railing's upright sufficiently."

She giggled, a high, horrible giggle.

I tried to draw on all my reserves of strength to rise to my feet and make a dash to safety from this mad woman, but as if she had read my mind, Lois gave me another contemptuous slap across the face, setting my head reeling once again.

I groaned with pain as I huddled against the cold, wet rock.

"When that failed, I tried to arrange another accident for you," went on Lois, and from her voice I knew that she was enjoying telling me her story, as she gloated over my current helplessness.

"The day we returned from Abbess Inch and you left me to sail the launch back to the boathouse, I cycled through Lower Tarris Woods to the Point, and managed to dislodge the main rung near the top of the rope rail. Then I hacked away a good bit of the track, so that the moment you set foot on it, it would give under you, and the loosened rope would be of no help, so that you would go plunging over the precipice. I had plenty of time to make a thorough job, because no one was likely to be out in the storm which had blown up, and see me near the path, and if anyone did call at my house and get no answer, they would take it for granted that I was sleeping off the shock of the afternoon.

"But again," she glared down at me, "you proved an impossible person to get rid of. This time, however, it will be different. This time you will not escape me. This time you will die. That old note, which Gavin once sent me, will have proved your invitation to death," she gloated. "And this time I will not kill you before the sea covers you over, so that there will be water in your lungs to prove your death an accident.

"Look behind you, Joanna Fraser. The tide is coming in fast. In a few minutes the waves will be all around you, drowning you, while I go safely home!"

She stood up, straight, and raised her sandbag high, ready to bring it crashing down on me for another stunning blow.

With a stupendous effort I rolled to one side as she swung her weapon towards me. She momentarily staggered off balance with the impetus of her blow, and with shaking limbs, I scrambled to my feet and started to stumble back across the sands to the path which led home.

Within seconds, Lois, her balance regained, was racing after me. I screamed with utter terror as I heard her footsteps close behind me, and my cry was echoed back from the land.

I looked up and saw two men come dashing out of the wood towards me, and seconds later Rory caught me firmly in his arms.

I clung to him hysterically, while he told me how his mother had found Gavin's note in my room, and meeting Gavin, who denied having sent it, they had both come running to the Pulpit.

His voice grew fainter and fainter, and then, with the sheer relief of knowing that I was safe in his arms, I let the unutterable weariness which was sweeping over me have its way.

Chapter Twenty-six

I lay in my bedroom at Tarris for three days, in a sort of twilight world of utter nervous exhaustion, unaware of what was going on around me; unaware that when Lois saw Rory and Gavin come racing to my rescue, she realized that her secret was out, and she had lost, and that all her hopes of a brilliant and glittering social future were over; that even if she had not already lost Gavin's love, she had now by her own cold-blooded actions forfeited it for all time.

With a hysterical laugh she had turned, her murderous sandbag still swaying wildly from her right hand, and ran out towards the incoming sea, plunging into the racing tidal waters with a final desolate cry.

Gavin had plunged in after her, and had almost been drowned himself in his attempt to save her.

For Grandfather's sake, the affair was given the minimum of publicity. The police, on investigating the few coherent remarks I had managed to make to them when they interrogated me on the afternoon of the tragedy, were satisfied that Lois had been guilty of Molly Mackay's murder, and responsible for the attempts on my life, and quietly closed their files on the case.

Everyone felt sorry for poor Mr Burgess, but surprisingly, it was from Gavin's mother that he was given the most help and comfort.

Gavin, miserable because Lois had read more into their past, brief flirtation than he had intended, postponed the announcement of his engagement to Sally Henderson, with whom he had, in between flirtations, been having an on-and-off affair for some years. It was Sally that Lois had mistaken me for when she had seen her with Gavin at the Pulpit.

But all these facts I learned later, because for the three days after Lois's death, all I did was lie dozing and dreaming, and my recurring dream was that Rory was constantly by my bedside, holding my hand.

I even dreamed that my mother and stepfather came into the room one night, and I smiled and said how glad I was that they had come to Tarris.

Then on the fourth day I woke up, and the world was sunlit, no longer a place of dreams and shadows, and Rory truly was there, by my bedside, holding my hand.

I squeezed his fingers with loving tightness, and smiled at him, shyly whispering his name.

His face lit up with a look of sparkling happiness.

"Joanna, my dear! How do you feel? You have given us all such a fright!" He tried to withdraw his hand, but with my returning strength I held it fast.

"Dear Rory," I whispered.

"Dear Rory!" he echoed the words in a sarcastic tone. "How can you call me that? If it hadn't been for me. If I hadn't summoned you to Tarrisdale, because I thought I was acting for the best, none of the frightening things which happened to you would have happened. How I wish I had not interfered with your life!"

"Do you really wish that, Rory?" I eased myself up to a sitting position, and still holding his strong, firm hand, I pressed it against my cheek. "Don't you realize that if you had not asked me to come to Tarrisdale, I would have gone off to Venice, and we might never have met?"

I pressed the palm of his hand against my lips. "Is that what you would have preferred?"

"Joanna!" My name was his exclamation of denial.

Forcibly he pulled his hand from mine, so that he could take me firmly in his arms, and as he held me close, my own arms circled his neck, and he pressed his cheeks against mine, till his lips found my mouth in a long, passionate kiss.

This time, my happy tears did not frighten him away, and he lovingly brushed them from my cheeks with caressing fingers, and said again softly the most important words of life, words which we were to repeat to each other over and over again in the long years together which lay ahead.

"Darling, I love you."